The
BLUFFER'S
GUIDE
to
THEATRE

The BLUFFER'S GUIDE

to

THEATRE

by **MICHAEL R. TURNER**

American Editor: **JOE SINGER**

Introduced by **DAVID FROST**

CROWN PUBLISHERS, INC., NEW YORK

© 1972 by Bluffer's Guides, Inc.

Library of Congress Catalog Card Number: 72–85727
ISBN: 0–517–500310

Inquiries should be addressed to Crown Publishers, Inc.
419 Park Avenue South, New York, N.Y. 10016.

Printed in the United States of America

Published simultaneously in Canada by General Publishing Company Limited

INTRODUCTION

OF ALL THE BREEDING grounds available to the pseudo-intellectual and that other social bird of prey, the intellectual snob, few are returned to as frequently as the theatre.

Perhaps it's because the territory is so especially lush for their particular needs, with a verdant undergrowth of personalities to be pecked away at and an abundance of perches to retreat to, if they are in the slightest danger of being pecked in return, and from which they can safely observe and shrill their call of derision.

And those calls are really shrill. For though you can never be sure where you will come across this particular species, and its plumage varies with the terrain—it might be wearing a five-hundred-dollar gown at a Broadway first night, jeans and a sweat shirt in a converted church, which itself sounds like a contradiction in terms in Greenwich Village, or sensible shoes at a rehearsal for an amateur performance in Duluth—there is one sure-fire giveaway: they are always very, very loud, and the wise man or woman will not try to outsquawk them.

In this respect they are the common grackle of the arts—they simply become deafeningly louder and increasingly repetitive and they won't easily let you escape once they realize they have stimulated a response from you.

But, like the grackle, they will fly off at the merest hint of an authority that's greater than their own, and though this book can only, and indeed, is only designed to, give you a working knowledge of the theatre, any one page of the facts it contains will be enough to send your pseud fluttering away in search of less dangerous meat and leave you free to enjoy the real magic, and the often equally magical anecdotes, of the theatre.

On television I have heard some wonderful stories from actors and performers about their experiences on stage—most of which, like so many great stories, were shattering to the performer when they happened but have become very funny with the healing passage of time.

Marty Brill told us one night about the heckler in a nightclub—because yes, nightclubs are theatre in their way—who'd supped rather

5

more wisely than well and who ordinarily would have been squelched with all due dispatch with lines like "Do you ever talk to your boss like that?" or "I don't care what your wife says to you when you switch off the light!"

But on this night the heckler was a woman. And though we might have finally got around to giving them increasingly equal pay and equal opportunity, there are still situations where a woman has to be handled, well, like a woman.

And this woman was good. Whatever response Marty made to her shouts from the audience she bettered. As he told it, she topped him every time. She was not only getting more laughs than he was, she was deserving them. Finally, in a not unnatural act of desperation he said: "Look, lady, why don't you pick on the band . . . there are ten of them . . . I'm just one guy on his own."

There was a pause, then back from the dark room she shouted: "Yeah? Well, you're a man short."

Marty survived to tell the tale and so did Richard Burton when he told us about the memorable St. David's Day performance of Henry IV, part I.

He had, before the performance, as was his habit on the celebration of the patron saint of Wales, consumed a rather large amount of beer. And once he'd got into his chain mail armor costume there was no getting out of it, nor indeed getting any part of him out of it, until the play was over . . . some three hours later, and well . . . as his co-star Sir Michael Redgrave observed when told afterwards what had really happened . . . "Oh, that's what it was, I thought you were sweating a lot during that fight scene."

But probably my favorite story about actors concerns one great English actor who is no longer with us and whose costar in a Shakespearean play was another celebrated English actor—who was also known by his partiality to a social drink or even ten before a performance.

And as the first actor made his entrance one night, a voice from the upper dress circle shouted down, "So and So, you're drunk."

And without a second's hesitation "So and So" shouted back, "If you think I'm drunk, wait till you see the Duke of Buckingham."

As a postscript, maybe you should jot down Sir Noel Coward's comment on one recent first night. A hundred people wanted to know what he had thought of it. Noel replied succinctly, "I think both the second act and the leading actor's throat should be cut."

DAVID FROST

WHOM ARE YOU TRYING
TO KID, ANYWAY?

WHAT TARGET HAVE YOU set yourself? Which theatre are you trying to infiltrate? There are many, but they can be divided for convenience into four—the tight, bitchy little world of the professional actor; the intense, dedicated theatre of the *avant-garde;* the real bluffer's jungle of the amateur; and that heady brew of the last two: university theatre.

This handy compendium can't possibly guide you over the threshold of all four, but you should know in advance those that are easier to enter than others, and the most difficult is recommended only to the really gifted and advanced bluffer.

To begin with, be warned that the most outwardly attractive to the true phony is by far the most dangerous. To mix on equal terms with professional stage people involves more than just dropping a few nicknames and knowing who is currently sleeping with whom. You would have to out-act the actors. For instance, you would be advised to cultivate the pallid, somewhat sickly complexion of those who habitually wear stage makeup. Ideally, you should drink in the right bars, eat at the right restaurants, and dance at the right nightclubs or discothèques: and that comes mighty expensive.

Perhaps your easiest way is via the local theatre group, and this guide assumes that this is your point of attack. To make your way here, spice your conversation with fashionable Continental names. You can be as phony as you like, provided you get the jargon right. The smart bluffer can achieve gratifying success, without having to write, act, direct, design, or sweep the stage, simply on the reputation—which no one will ever want to question—of having translated into Lallans one act of a play by Arrabal.

Your aim, of course, may be humbler. If you want to impress the peasants in the local community Center Drama Group, success is within easy grasp. But there are risks. Even if you aren't forced to participate in their productions, you may have to sit through them. Only the very brave could face that, and I would recommend your joining that particular branch of the amateur theatre known as the "shamateurs." These worthy devotees of Thespis have a splendid belief in their honest unprofessionalism, a belief that because they act for the love of it, their uncommercial fervor is somehow more to be admired than the efforts of actors who actually have to earn their bread by it. These are dedicated theatre folk who seldom see the professional theatre, but who, when not acting themselves, go to other shamateur productions to criticize everything, often audibly, during the course of the play.

Finally you might like to attempt the most socially acceptable, perhaps the most enjoyable, and certainly the silliest theatre of all: university drama. For success here, however, it is advisable to be either an undergraduate or a freewheeling professor. So, gentle bluffer, unless you are already among their ranks, you will have to talk your way into a university as well as into the theatre.

But it may be that you just want to impress ordinary people in bars or at parties by your racy theatrical presence. If so, a quick glance through this book, the acquisition of a few nicknames, and a copy of *Variety* under your arm will see you through. But take note of the short but true story that follows.

A rather lively party was nearing its climax, and a group of young and admiring ladies was reacting in the most gratifying fashion to the backstage gossip of a gentleman bluffer. He was giving a graphic account of his amorous exploits in the arms of a currently fashionable actress—let us call her Miss Jones. "And next morning," concluded the bluffer, "I just couldn't get rid of her. All over me. Quite a girl." "How fascinating," remarked the smallest and most mouselike of his audience, "Really fascinating. Particularly as I happen to be Miss Jones."

JARGON

THE FIRST STEP IN YOUR initiation is to equip yourself with the essential jargon, so that you know that stage braces hold up scenery, not your daughter's teeth, and that dropping the asbestos is not a clumsiness by the wardrobe mistress. The next few sections are spiced with a little history so that you get your jargon in depth.

THE THEATRE BUILDING

You must always give the impression that the theatre is your home, tossing off terms like "tabs" or "flies" or "cyc" with easy and slightly weary aplomb.

A rapid tour backstage will now follow, and the theatre we are visiting is old-fashioned and Victorian, full of plush and gilt and cherubs and buxom nymphs grasping the masks of comedy and tragedy, and rich, red curtains. Nowadays, of course, the idea of a theatre for innocent thrills and amusement is frowned upon in all progressive circles and a modern auditorium is apt to look like an exhibition piece by a firm of steel scaffolding specialists, all tastefully done over in black and various shades of mud. There will be more on this subject later, but as most technical words and phrases derive from the last century or even earlier, we must trot briskly through a conventional proscenium theatre first of all.

The proscenium arch (or *pros arch,* or plain *pros*)—there's a word, incidentally, that goes right back to ancient Rome—is just the picture frame separating the auditorium from the stage. *Picture-frame theatre* is a useful phrase, to be expressed in tones of distaste in *avant-garde* circles, for the traditional arrangement of auditorium divided from the stage by a curtain. In the seventies, it is the task of the up-to-date architect to avoid having a proscenium in his theatre at all and to build, by the most advanced methods, all the disadvantages of an Elizabethan innyard into a modern structure.

Hanging in the proscenium are the *tableau curtains* or *house tabs,* or *tabs,* or *act drop* (now you can begin to grasp just how tiresome learning about the theatre is going to be. All these terms mean the same thing). They are raised and lowered by motors and counterweights, or just cranked up and down by brute force. Only movie theatres and school auditoriums, as a rule, have tabs drawn from the side.

Just inside the proscenium, in front of the tabs, is lowered the *safety curtain* or *asbestos,* made of incombustible material with a steel framework. To "drop the asbestos," therefore, is simply to lower the safety curtain.

Let us now go from the auditorium through the *pass door,* also fireproof, and onto the stage. The first thing you will notice is the smell: behind all the glitter and glamor is the unmistakable and powerful aroma of dust and glue sizing. There is normally a pretty sharp draft, too.

Look up, and you will see a tangle of ropes and wires, acres of canvas stirring gently in that breeze, and a jungle of lighting equipment. This cavernous area above you is called the *flies,* and from here scenery is dropped into position on the stage floor. Right in the roof is the hefty steel framework, the *gridiron,* or more usually *grid,* with the pulleys from which the scenery and lights are suspended by ropes and steel cables, the *lines.* On either side of the stage, halfway up the walls, are the *fly floors,* galleries where husky *flymen* tighten up or slacken the lines to raise and lower the suspended scenery. On larger or better equipped stages, human muscle is replaced by counterweights.

Now look down. In older theatres the stage floor is likely to be raked, or sloped, rising from the front to the back wall—hence the terms *downstage,* meaning the front of the stage near the audience, and *upstage,* at the back, away from the audience. When one actor upstages another, the oldest, easiest, and most selfish way of dominating a rival, he is simply placing himself nearer the back of the stage so that his companion has to turn away from the audience to face him. It has been known for two famous and temperamental actresses to upstage each other with such determination that they finished by playing most of their scenes together right up against the back wall of the scenery.

Above and *below* are terms of similar origin from the days of the raked stage. One actor is above another if he is upstage of him.

Stage left and right are the actor's left and right, not the audience's. Ignorance of this simple rule has caused badly briefed bluffers acute embarrassment before now.

At this point, you should be able to grasp what is meant by "down left," "up right," and so on, but a little plan of the acting area will help the slow ones among us:

back wall

up right	up center	up left
UR	UC	UL
right	center	left
R	C	L
down right	down center	down left
DR	DC	DL

front of stage

If, however, you want to be really exact, you can go even further:

back wall

up right	up right center	up center	up left center	up left
UR	URC	UC	ULC	UL
right	right center	center	left center	left
R	RC	C	LC	L
down right	down right center	down center	down left center	down left
DR	DRC	DC	DLC	DL

front of stage

Now, to compound the confusion, we come to the terms *on* and *off*. When an actor moves *on,* he is going "onstage" from the side toward the center. Vice versa, of course, for *off. Offstage* is out of the acting area in the wings, in the dressing room, or in the street outside.

Back to the floor of the stage. Beneath your feet you may see *traps* (trapdoors). Through one variety, the *star trap,* the demon king would appear in a flash and a cloud of smoke, and sunk to chest height in another, the *grave trap,* the grave digger in *Hamlet* cracks the unfunniest jokes in English literature.

On really lavish stages, whole sections of the floor can be raised and lowered on hydraulic jacks. Quite modest theatres are likely to have a *revolve* in the center of the stage. This can be used to help change scenery: large and heavy constructions can be twirled around with ease, and no producer of a revue can leave the revolve alone.

Downstage, on the edge facing the audience, are the *footlights*. These, which light the house tabs in that traditionally thrilling moment before the curtain rises, are now looked upon as very old hat. They are a relic of the candles and later the gas flares of early theatres, and are completely banished from many modern stages.

As you face the audience, on your left and right are the sides of the stage, the *wings*. The prompter sits or stands in either the right or left wing. On the Continent and in opera houses in this country the prompter is apt to live in a little box with a hood over him in the center of the front edge of the stage.

In the corner against the proscenium wall is the stage manager's desk, or *board*. From here, like a pilot in the cockpit of a Boeing, he controls everything during a performance by means of switches, buttons, colored lights, and bells. Here he rings up the curtain and is rude on the telephone to his fellow technicians or the house manager in the auditorium. When you are onstage, the auditorium is known as the front of house, and *out front* just means "in the audience."

The back wall of the stage may just be an expanse of brickwork decorated with fire hoses and exhortations to keep quiet, but in some theatres it may be plastered smooth and perhaps curved. When lit from above, this can represent the sky, and is called the *cyclorama*, or *cyc* for short. Occasionally you see cycloramas made of canvas which are prone to wrinkles, spoiling any illusion.

THE OPEN STAGE ARENA THEATRE, THEATRE-IN-THE-ROUND, AND ALL THAT

When you begin to pontificate about how vital the open stage is to theatrical health, you ought to know a bit about how this wonder cure started.

As I mentioned earlier, the modern theatre man tends to despise the old-fashioned Georgian and Victorian theatre form of proscenium or picture-frame stage. Closer *contact* (use this word continually) is what is wanted nowadays—probably because, in the twentieth century, the movies and television can outdo the "picture" or or spectacular aspect of the theatre. So back we go to the Elizabethans.

In Tudor days, plays were performed on a simple wooden platform at one end of an innyard with galleries round the sides. When the theatrical companies of Shakespeare's time began to put up buildings specifically to house plays, they modeled them pretty closely on the innyard. A few refinements were added, like a roof over the stage to keep the rain off the actors—or, to be more precise, off their expensive costumes; the common mob of the audience milling around in the *pit* (what was originally the yard floor) just got wet. If you, the affluent theatregoer, could afford a penny or so more, you would buy a place on a bench in one of the galleries that ringed the "wooden 0."

With the audience on three sides of it, here was the true open or *apron* stage, and there is little doubt that actors and audience exchanged comments and that the contact was physical on occasions.

At the back of the stage was a curtained recess, where a few rudimentary pieces of scenery were probably used to suggest a setting. On the Continent and at court, lavish scenery was the rule. To gain the full effect of expensive staging, the nobility sat at one end of a hall and the performers orated, danced, and sang on a platform at the other end. Behind the actors was a picture frame (which had evolved from the center entrance of the stage façade of the old Roman theatre) containing elaborate scenery. In England, the masque was produced in this fashion.

Cromwell and his not-so-merry men banned the theatre altogether for general sinfulness. The Restoration restored more than the monarchy: it brought back the wicked old theatre, which reappeared as a blend of the old popular theatre of the Elizabethans and Jacobeans, and the procenium form used at court. The actors performed on the front part of the stage, and the area behind the picture frame was reserved for scenery. As time went on, the actors moved back to join the scenery, and the *forestage* that originally jutted out into the audience gradually receded farther and farther into the proscenium, until in the eighteenth century it was just a few feet deep, and then in the next century withered away altogether.

Professional stage people were perfectly satisfied with their picture-frame illusionist theatres of the end of Victoria's reign, despite the many limitations. But a new kind of theatre man appeared: the intellectual, the theorist. Within a few years a revolution of ideas was in progress, and the first name the bluffer should commit to memory is that of *William Poel*. Shakespeare was currently produced in the most complicated and gorgeous manner, with tons of meticulously painted scenery; Poel returned to the simple open stage of the Elizabethan innyard for his productions of plays of that period. Other theorists followed Poel, notably *Jacques Copeau* in France, who worked with an open stage in his own theatre, the Vieux Colombier, from 1913 onward.

Plain, direct contact between actors and audience were the aims of Poel and Copeau; basically opposed to them were other famous theorists of the time, such as *Edward Gordon Craig* and *Adolphe Appia*. Craig, the brilliant and wayward illegitimate son of Ellen Terry, the actress, and Appia, a Swiss, saw the actor as a puppet in a theatre of visual effect, where dance, mime, monolithic scenery, and atmospheric lighting were paramount. Their theories were based on only a handful of actual productions: magnificent ideas but very difficult to translate into practical theatre terms. In fact, Craig and Appia are chiefly important more for what they said than for what they actually did.

The idea of the open or *arena* stage caught on in a big way only after the second World War. America theatre people took it up with enthusiasm, and the experiments proliferated. *Theatre-in-the-round* is the fashionable phrase. You should let the uninformed know that it's at least twenty years old.

Theatre-in-the-round involves having the audience on *all* sides of the actors. Plays are staged on a central platform or in just a circle or a square marked on the floor. This means that the unfortunate spectator has to enjoy large sections of the play spoken with the cast's backs to him. He is usually so close to the acting area that characters onstage are inclined to trip over his feet, and because of the problems of lighting an island stage, he is likely to have a couple of spotlights glaring straight into his eyes.

Nevertheless, the arena stage, with the audience distributed two-thirds or three-quarters the way round the acting area, is still going great guns. Although it avoids the worst excesses of theatre-in-the-round, it is still quite difficult for the director to manage and doesn't suit all kinds of plays—realistic late-nineteenth-century dramas, meant by their authors to be staged with meticulous attention to naturalistic detail, work awkwardly on an open stage.

Although proscenium-type theatres are still being built, most of them can be adapted for open stage productions.

Anyway, by now we are a long way from the crimson plush and tarnished gilt of the Victorian playhouse, from the old illusionistic stage, and the bluffer will be suitably contemptuous of the style of theatre that evolved from that period. You must, nevertheless, pick your company carefully when approving the open stage: many professional actors—the theatre is the most conventional of professions—have a very natural attachment to old methods. Anyone who has gone through a theatre school in the last ten years, however, is likely to be a firm convert.

A thought, though. You could be so *avant-garde* as to be enthusiastic in praise of the proscenium theatre, knowing that the fashion pendulum will swing the other way eventually—but this is not going to happen for a long time yet.

SCENERY

Not only will you have to seem to know your way about the theatre building, you should also be able to drop the odd technical word now and again about scenery.

Once more, we'll start with the oldest forms. *Backcloths* and *skycloths* are self-explanatory: these large areas of canvas painted with scenes—or in the case of skycloths, quite plain—are dropped into position onstage from the flies. A cloth framing the whole stage, with the center removed, and the onstage edges representing, say, foliage, is called a *cut cloth*. A *gauze* is precisely what it sounds like: with clever lighting it's used for transformation scenes, in which an apparently solid wall dissolves before your astonished eyes. It is all a matter of lighting the gauze from in front to begin with, then fading that illumination out and bringing up the lights on the scene behind. The more satisfactory expedient than a skycloth for representing the limitless depths of the heavens—the cyclorama—has already been mentioned.

To mask the sides of the stage in theatres in the seventeenth and eighteenth centuries were *wings*, sliding in grooves on and off.

These would be painted in perspective to represent walls or, with jagged edges, trees and bushes. Wings no longer run in grooves. Curtains hanging from the flies at the sides of the stage and doing service as wings are called *legs*. Just inside the proscenium arch on either side are narrow wings, generally painted black, the *tormentors*. Often inside the main proscenium you will find another, perhaps cutting down the size of the pros opening. This second pros is the *false procenium*.

Nowadays, in progressive productions it is *de rigueur* to dispense with borders and even wings so that the customers can get a good view of all the untidy lighting equipment and other viscera that the stage designer once went to great lengths to keep decently hidden. Thus the spectator is constantly reminded that he is in a theatre— as if he were ever likely to forget it—and not be deluded into thinking that what he sees on the stage is real life. This is all part of the alienation effect that Brecht went after.

Most scenery representing rooms or walls onstage is composed of flats: framed areas of canvas. They may be hinged together, or more often lashed one to the other with *lash lines* tied off on *cleats*. They are kept firmly in position by means of *stage braces* and weights. Windows (without glass, which would cause unsightly reflections from the powerful lights) and doors, usually like the real thing, are fitted into flats. The flats that stand behind these, providing a view of the Alps or a glimpse of the billiard room, are called *backings*. The complete setting of a room composed of flats, perhaps with a ceiling lowered from the flies, is a *box set*.

Often you will see long pieces of scenery with cut-out edges doing duty as distant hills, or hedges, or a street of buildings: these are *ground rows*. *Set pieces* are single bits of scenery, like a tree, a statue, or a building by itself. Stairs and steps are used, of course, a great deal, rising to folding platforms called rostrums. In a university theatre you are likely to hear learned people call more than one rostrum "rostra."

In big theatres a whole set can be rolled onstage from the wings, on a table.

There is one fashionable stage designer whom you should re-member to throw into the conversation. Pick one out of the current crop. You can easily see who is fashionable by reading a few reviews.

LIGHTING

No bluffer should try to pretend that he knows anything about the technicalities of lighting. A vague intimation that he knows how to use it is enough. He can, and should, say that it is far more important than scenery, and that the most rewarding productions of Shakespeare he has seen have been those on a completely bare stage, the whole mood of the play having been conveyed by subtle lighting.

As the equipment used by lighting men advances steadily into the misty regions of higher electronics, their mystique likewise grows to demigod levels. But signs of a reaction may be visible.

The sensible bluffer, however, will get acquainted with the names of the more obvious pieces of equipment.

We begin with what are termed, in splendid Victorian fashion for this most contemporary of arts, the *lanterns*. The spotlight or *spot* has a narrow beam that can be focused; it comes in several varieties, but the most efficient forms are *mirror spots*. In all theatres you will see spots fixed to the front of the circle, in the ceiling, and in housings at the sides of the auditorium: these are the F.O.H. spots (front of the house). All these lanterns have hard-edged, precise beams; call them *profile spots* if you want to sound really professional.

Out front, incidentally, may be high-powered *following* or *follow spots*, living in a little room high up at the back of the auditorium. These are used to follow the movement of the star about the stage, and once upon a time they were magnificently spluttering *lime lights*, or later, arc lights. In any case, they are likely to be given the generic title of *limes*.

Hanging above the stage on lengths of steel piping called *bars* you will see many spots, most of them today with a large lens, ribbed in concentric circles, the *Fresnel spots*, providing a wider, softer beam than the profile spots. Also hanging up there you will see *floods*, which are basically just metal boxes containing a bulb. Rows of small floods built together in one long unit are called *box battens*, or simply *battens* for short. They are numbered from the proscenium No. 1 batten, No. 2 batten, and so on, to the *cyc batten* lighting the cyclorama, or perhaps a skycloth. The spot bars are numbered in the same way, too. Box battens giving flat areas of light are now old-fashioned. Those amateurs who don't know any better or who can't afford any better are devoted to them. They are anathema to the shamateur. *Footlights,* often missing from progressive theatres, are just box battens on the floor.

The *switchboard* controlling all this equipment is to be found on a platform at the side of the stage, or perhaps on the fly floor of old theatres. In modern buildings it is more likely to be in a room, often doubling as a projection box, at the back of the auditorium, so that the electrician can see the immediate effects of pressing the wrong switch.

The waxing and waning of stage lights is accomplished by means of *dimmers.* Nowadays the old, bulky mechanical dimmers are being replaced by *thyristor* dimmers and similar electronic devices developed for TV studios. The control desk for such systems, including remote controls, memories, and preset keys, remind one of organ consoles.

JOBS IN THE THEATRE

This is a particular important section, for unless the bluffer knows who is who in the theatre, he is likely to make a fatal slip and give the whole game away.

This is the way it works on Broadway. The *producer* is the one who puts the whole package together. He options the script from the playwright; he arranges for the financing from the *backers* or *angels;* he engages the cast and the creative people; he rents the theatre and sets a date for the opening. In the old days, producers used their own money to put on shows. Today, a producer is paid so much per week for expenses for which he supplies his own services, those of a *production secretary*, and a telephone. After the investors have been paid their share, the producer is entitled to fifty percent of the profits. In Europe, a producer is usually called the *manager.*

If an angel puts up enough money of his own or is able to bring in outside investors, he may be occasionally designated an *associate* or an *assistant producer.*

Serving right under the producer is the *general manager.* This is the guy who does all the dirty work while the producer is giving out interviews and performing all the other public relations duties. He negotiates with the various unions (everyone on Broadway from the director to the porter belongs to a union); he negotiates the contracts; he hires the crew; he shops around for the theatre; he arranges for the costumes and scenery; in short, he supervises every commercial and financial aspect of the show. He is usually hired by the producer three or more months before the opening, and he draws a weekly salary.

The *director* is the fellow who makes it all happen on stage. He joins the producer and author in casting the show, he stages the action, he artistically supervises the costumes, scenery, lighting (book, music, lyrics, and dances in a musical), and so on. His job ends when the show opens. Technically, he is supposed to check out the performance periodically (assuming there is a long run), but some directors don't bother and the shows sometimes deteriorate in time. The director is one of the first creative people engaged and he is usually paid a flat fee in advance in addition to a percentage of the weekly gross receipts.

Serving under the director is the *stage manager* (sometimes called the production stage manager). Union rules require two stage managers for musicals and three for straight plays. This is one of the most exacting jobs in the theatre, since the stage manager must heed or supervise every creative and technical aspect of the production before the opening night through to its final performance. He makes sure that the director's orders are carried out; he sees to it that the actors, electricians, and stagehands are functioning properly; he sits with the prompt book through every performance and gives the light cues; he supervises the hanging of the show (the placing of scenery and lighting); he makes sure the actors are ready to perform and sees to it that they get off and on at the right time and in the right place.

He must also rehearse and direct the replacements, and generally see to it that everyone is where he belongs and doing that for which he is paid.

The stage manager is given one or more assistants called A.S.M.'s. The stage managers are hired a few weeks before rehearsals begin and continue with the show to its bitter end. They are paid a weekly salary.

Occasionally, there is someone called a *production supervisor,* but this vague term can be applied to a stage manager or to some outside person who is brought in to assist the director.

The *company manager* works under the general manager and is the producer's business representative in the theatre during the run of the show. He is usually hired a month prior to opening and has a variety of responsibilities. He makes up the weekly payroll for the company, he checks the box office to see how many tickets have been sold, he pays the producer's bills—in short, he takes care of a particular show's financial considerations for the general manager who may be supervising two or three shows at the same time.

The *house manager* works for the owner of the theatre and is responsible for the operation of the house itself. He supervises the house staff, which includes the ushers, the backstage doorman, the porters, the box office personnel, the engineer, and the usual stage-hands that are assigned to that particular house.

The *treasurer* is in charge of the box office. He has two or more assistants and a *mail order girl* who answer the phone and sorts the mail orders.

The two *porters* take turns serving as the *front doorman,* who usually fetches the reservations from the box office for the waiting customers. They also clean the house between performances.

The other creative people hired by the producer for the show may include a *scenic designer,* a *costume designer,* a *lighting designer,* and a *composer, lyricist, choreographer* (if the show is a musical). They are paid fees plus a weekly percentage, which varies with every production.

There is also a *press agent* who is paid a weekly salary, various lawyers and accountants, etc.

The crew hired for the show may vary from four to forty stage-hands, depending upon the complexity of the scenery, the variety of offstage sounds, or other technical problems. These are carpenters, flymen, electricians, and *property men.* There is a *wardrobe mistress* who is in charge of the costumes and *dressers* who help the stars put on and take off their clothes.

Back to the creative end. Each *musical* Broadway house is obliged to keep a number of *musicians* on salary whether the theatre is engaged or dark. These gentlemen are known as *walkers.* When a show comes in, the producer engages a *contractor* to hire the additional musicians for the performance.

Musicals may also require one or many of the following specialists: *orchestrators, copyists, arrangers, hair stylists, dance music composers,* and the like.

ACTING IN THE SIXTIES: STANISLAVSKI, THE METHOD, AND HAPPENINGS

THE ACTOR'S TRAINING is a long one, and as the bluffer's very last intention is actually (perish the thought) to appear on a stage before an audience, he need only know of the current cults.

We have to go back a bit, to Russia at the turn of the century, to meet the prophet of all modern acting, Konstantin Stanislavski. Your bookshelf, incidentally, should carry copies of his holy writ, *An Actor Prepares* and *Building a Character.*

Stanislavski must never be questioned, except by an avowed disciple of Bertolt Brecht. He is supreme as the master teacher of naturalistic acting.

Stanislavski was a director who helped found the Moscow Art Theatre. He reacted against the ham acting of the time, the expansive melodramatic style of stock gestures, sonorous voice, overemphasized enunciation, all of which had no subtlety or relation to how people spoke or moved in real life. To do them justice, the actors of that time had little other than crude scripts to work from, frequently inattentive audiences to dominate, and no director to weld the play into a whole, only a stage manager to see that the actors did not bump into each other in rehearsal.

Such hack styles might have worked with plays in which situation and broadly drawn character were all-important, but were useless when delicate atmosphere had to be created, say, in the new plays of Chekhov.

What Stanislavski taught was minute attention to naturalistic detail, extensive training and rehearsal lasting months for a single play, and the careful shading of voice and gesture. Suggestion was more important than statement. As his style developed, Stanislavski insisted more and more that the actor immerse himself in his part, sinking into the psychological state of the character.

Stanislavski's system led to the development of the *Method*. The Method as practiced by the *New York Actors Studio* under Lee Strasberg sank the actor into his part completely. The basic difference between Stanislavski and the Method is that the former always insisted that the actor's part should be subordinate to the whole production, whereas in the Method, the complete identification of the actor with his role is everything.

Methods used in teaching the Method include *improvisation* and a great number of demanding physical exercises.

Names that are associated with the Method are, of course, the legendary James Dean and Marlon Brando, and the directors Lee Strasberg and Elia Kazan.

A word about improvisation. This is the technique of the actor's creating his own part, either by mime or by mime and dialogue. An essential part of the training at any school of acting nowadays, it assumed enormous importance for the Method, and in many productions by advanced directors it helps write the play itself. Whole plays have been improvised, one an experiment by William Saroyan, the result bearing the title of *Sam, the Highest Jumper of Them All.*

Happenings have no plot, they are simply events, usually as noisy as possible, occurring at random and without premeditation. They are the theatrical equivalents of action painting and in their many varieties they hail from New York and San Francisco.

Examples of this delightful art form are *Poem for Table, Chairs and Benches* performed in California, consisting of the noise made by furniture being pushed around the floor; or an event consisting of a gong scraping for an hour or so over cement; or general smashing up of any objects that come to hand.

READING MATTER

NATURALLY, YOU WILL WANT to carry around the right magazines and papers. A few years ago it would have been easier when *Theatre Arts* was still being published, keeping us up to the minute with what to think, what to approve of, and what to sniff at. Get the back numbers if you can, and leave them casually about your pad. It will show that you bluff in depth.

You will subscribe to *Variety, Show Business, Billboard, Dance Magazine, The Drama Review, Backstage,* and *Theatre Crafts.*

THE "ISMS"

THE VITAL PART OF THE bluffer's equipment, if he is to keep his end up in the *avant-garde* theatre, is a nodding acquaintance with the main names of twentieth-century drama. A lot of them fit fairly neatly under the "isms" before the last war, and the "theatres"—of cruelty, the absurd, etc.—since then. Let us now take a very deep breath and launch out into:

REALISM

A vigorous movement of the late nineteenth century, with Ibsen as the most notable exponent. There isn't space to deal with Henrik here (dip into any history of the drama), but you should know that his idea—and that of the other realists—was to replace the conventional flamboyance of melodrama and the artificiality of the *well-made play* with dramas that looked like real life. Incidentally, you should treasure the phrase "well-made play": it applies to the carefully constructed social dramas of Augustin Eugène Scribe and

Victorien Sardou in France and Arthur Wing Pinero in Britain. There are signs of a revival of interest in their well-carpentered, mechanical work, so make the most of it.

A great disciple of Ibsen and high seriousness was George Bernard Shaw, who is becoming fashionable again but with a strong period flavor. Like most theatrical movements, realism was carried to extremes, and it turned into:

NATURALISM

Naturalism was so ultrarealistic that it tried to put on the stage all the more horrid aspects of human life. Well-washed actors performed with terrific attention to detail the depredations of bedbugs, lice, fleas, starvation, and alcoholism. There has always been a *nostalgie pour la boue* in the theatre, and naturalism is apt to crop up all over the place.

During the naturalistic craze, a style and method of acting was born under the aegis of Konstantin Stanislavski, and you will find details of the trouble he started later.

Dramatists to note—they were preceded, by the way, by Émile Zola with his nice line in vice and crime—include the Russian Maxim Gorky (author of *The Lower Depths*), Gerhart Hauptmann (who wrote *Rose Bernd* and *Die Ratten*), and the gloomy but important Swede, August Strindberg (like Ibsen, he's too big for treatment here). Naturalists as a school tended to get misty at the edges and evolve into symbolists and expressionists.

SYMBOLISM

In many ways a reaction against naturalism. It was in full spate by the end of the last century and presented in symbols the drama of the human soul. Sometimes it was very, very beautiful—as with Maurice Maeterlinck's children's play, *The Bluebird*—sometimes powerful, as in Ibsen's last works, and it was certainly invariably sad, like the dreams of the dying girl in *Hanneles Himmelfahrt* (*Hannele's Journey to Heaven*) by Gerhart Hauptmann.

Came the first World War, which shattered theatre intellectuals, as well as the rest of society, and set in train a whole succession of isms.

DADAISM

Dadaism reacted against everything, and the desire to shock was paramount. The splendid iconoclast Tristan Tzara, who described his play, *Le Coeur à Gaz*, as "the biggest swindle of the century in three acts," started it all in 1916. Dada didn't produce much of note for the theatre—most of its eccentric fire was reserved for writing, typography, and painting—but it is certainly a handy cult word for the bluffer. "Dada," incidentally, is supposed to come from the baby's first utterance.

In the twenties Dada flared on, but eventually petered out into surrealism and expressionism.

SURREALISM

Like Dada, surrealism flowered mainly in the visual arts. It influenced the expressionist theatre a good deal, but produced little worthwhile drama of its own. A presurrealist of immense quotability for the bluffer, however, is Alfred Jarry, and you will find something about him under the Theatre of the Absurd.

EXPRESSIONISM

Expressionism germinated in the German theatre at the turn of the century and produced luxuriant and curious blooms in the twenties.

In expressionism the action on the stage represented psychological conflicts, the frenzied goings-on in man's soul. Every character was heavily symbolic, and humor, when it did appear at all, as in *The Insect Play* by Karel and Josef Čapek, was usually far from jolly— usually harsh and scarifying. The despair, disillusionment, and hysteria of postwar Europe flooded the stage.

The expressionist theatre was a paradise for director and designer, and the actor was often used as a puppet (*see* Mechanism).

The forerunner of the expressionists in the early nineteenth century was Georg Büchner, the author of *Dantons Tod* (*Danton's Death*), which is becoming very fashionable. Another Büchner play to be noted is *Woyzeck* (on which Alban Berg based his opera *Wozzek*). Strindberg was another early expressionist with such plays as *The Ghost Sonata,* and so was Frank Wedekind, a very *in* name at the moment since his main preoccupation was sex, in *Spring's Awakening* and other violent dramas. Both Strindberg and Wedekind are pre-first World War, and none of those that followed, with the exception of Brecht, came close to their standards as playwrights.

The three main expressionist Germans of the twenties are Ernst Toller, author of *Masse Mensch* (*Masses and Men*), Walter Hasenclever, who wrote *Antigone,* and Georg Kaiser, whose best play is the spectacular *Gas.* Bertolt Brecht can be counted as an expressionist in his early years, but more about him later.

MECHANISM

Just a matter of making actors behave like machines. Indeed in this branch of expressionism the ideal was for actors to be replaced by machines altogether.

THEATRICALISM

A director's movement in Germany and, especially Russia, a reaction against the naturalistic productions of Stanislavski. Its chief figure was a Russian director, Alexander Tairov.

FORMALISM

An extension of theatricalism, involving intense stylization of acting, design, and production. *Vsevolod Meyerhold* was the leading formalist director.

SOCIALIST REALISM

As you can guess, this was another Russian movement. It was supposed to represent a true revolutionary theatre; it extolled the virtues of the Communist state and poked rather clumsy fun at aristocrats and bourgeois. It was (of course) a reaction against formalism.

The plays of Vladimir Mayakovski, although they had formalist productions by Mayakovski, could be classed under socialist realism. *The Bedbug* is his best-known work.

OUTSIDE THE "ISMS"

THERE WAS CERTAINLY more frenetic experiment in the twenties than at any time before or since, but many mainstream playwrights were only slightly attacked by the isms, or were infected first by one then by another, and they are listed in this section.

Such dramatists as Bernard Shaw, Sean O'Casey, and Noel Coward only occasionally used expressionist elements in their usually realistic writing. J. B. Priestley woke up to expressionism in the thirties and after, and used the style in warm, misty plays like *Johnson Over Jordan.*

Americans, as usual, showed more liveliness, with Elmer Rice and Eugene O'Neill to a lesser extent trying to break conventional bonds. O'Neill's ambitious dramas deal with big, emotional themes, and you should quote *The Hairy Ape* (which is expressionist), *Desire Under the Elms,* the immense Civil War drama based on the Greek Orestes myth, *Mourning Becomes Electra,* and *The Iceman Cometh.* There is Elmer Rice's *Adding Machine,* a kind of morality play, with the hero called Mr. Zero.

Social consciousness hit the States in the thirties, and political plays about strikebreakers, revolting garment workers, exploited blacks, and fascism were all the rage for a while. In addition to Rice, Clifford Odets (*Waiting for Lefty*), Maxwell Anderson (*Key Largo*), and Sinclair Lewis (*It Can't Happen Here*) are worth remembering.

Back in England, political protest got mixed up with a new poetic school. W. H. Auden and Christopher Isherwood wrote essentially half-baked satirical verse dramas such as *The Ascent of F6.* More muscular new talent arrived with *Murder in the Cathedral* by T. S. Eliot. His distinctive brand of intellectual free verse persisted into the forties and fifties with *The Cocktail Party* and other plays, but Eliot was a literary rather than a theatrical figure.

A shower of poetic sparks was thrown off by Christopher Fry in the early fifties: *The Lady's Not for Burning* sounded brilliant at first hearing, but Fry was drunk with colorful metaphor. His short vogue in the theatre was abruptly truncated by the emergence of the Angry Young Men.

More vital work appeared in France in the thirties, and two major dramatists, Jean Giraudoux and Jean Anouilh, whose reputations are now a trifle faded, reached their peak during the war and after.

Jean Giraudoux wrote in firm, sophisticated, poetic prose, and his antiwar comedy *Tiger at the Gates* (Christopher Fry's title for his translation of *La Guerre de Troie n'aura pas lieu—The Trojan War Will Not Take Place*) will certainly live. *Duel of Angels,* his last play, written in the forties, shows how dangerous innocence and purity can be for the world. This philosophy is also typical of Anouilh, who achieved more popular success than Giraudoux.

Anouilh is a magnificent theatrical craftsman, but the bluffer will follow current fashion by acknowledging that fact condescendingly and also denigrating him as shallow and sentimental. He is very important, nonetheless, if only as a figure to be sniped at. Anouilh's plays are divided into five groups: *Pièces roses,* the comedies: *Pièces noires,* the tragedies; *Pièces grinçantes,* harsh plays; *Pièces brillantes,* the later glittering comedies; and *Pièces costumées,* costumed plays.

Use the phrase "Anouilh heroine" to describe the waif who looks innocent but who is patiently disillusioned and experienced. She is a representative of that cynical whimsicality of his that works superbly well in performance but doesn't bear close examination. Typical of Anouilh's earlier style are *Ring Round the Moon,* a soufflé-light comedy about twin brothers, one good and one wicked, and *Antigone,* a tragedy about the pointlessness of idealism. Of more recent plays, his version of the St. Joan story, his popular but facile *Becket,* and *Poor Bitos,* in which aristocrats torture a self-made man as cruel as themselves, stand out.

Anouilh is the classic case of the writer who got too successful with his audiences to please the intellectuals.

Jean-Paul Sartre and Jean Cocteau both wrote a number of plays. Sartre's are tough, singularly effective essays on the themes of his own famous philosophy, existentialism. *Huis Clos (No Exit)* is a nightmarish picture of three people torturing one another eternally after death: man alone is responsible for his own tragedy, and "hell is other people." A later play of Sartre's is the much-praised *The Condemned of Altona,* a drama about guilt in Germany after the war, but applicable equally to Algeria, Ireland, or any country where human greed has brought large-scale misery.

Cocteau, once the darling of the intellectuals, has faded badly. He experimented with most of the isms, flitted from poetry to plays to films to design and back again. His obsessive theme, love and death, is invariably presented with a chic French romanticism in works like *The Eagle Has Two Heads, La Belle et la Bête,* and *Orphée,* the last two being splendidly Gothic films.

Now we come to one name the bluffer must remember, Luigi Pirandello. His principal subject is the dance of illusion and reality, and it is brought out most effectively in his famous play, *Six Characters in Search of an Author,* first produced in 1921. Actors who are rehearsing an earlier play of Pirandello's *The Rules of the Game,* are interrupted by six individuals who claim that they are the people created by the author and that they want to finish the play themselves. Each has his own idea about how this should be done, and their versions of the same events are very different. Other plays of Pirandello to be quoted are *Henry IV* and *Right You Are, If You Think You Are.* His importance, you will say, lies not so much in his dramatic skill as in his presentation of the pointlessness of life and the uncertainty of reality that looks ahead to the Theatre of the Absurd.

He influenced Ugo Betti, another Italian, who can be called Pirandello's successor. Betti's themes are responsibility and identity, and his best play so far, *The Burnt Flower Bed,* has as its protagonist a politician, a man who ruins his family's life by allowing ends to justify means.

A more effective poetic dramatist than T. S. Eliot was Federico García Lorca, a young Spaniard killed in the Civil War. *Blood Wedding* consists of savage goings-on among the peasantry, highly symbolic and with magnificent poetry mixed with bad. *The House of Bernarda Alba* is his best play: poetic prose is the medium here, used with great theatrical power. Again, violence and high passion rage, this time in the house of a matriarch where her five daughters are fighting to be free of her domination.

Two Americans now. Tennessee Williams began with the delicately impressionistic and symbolic play, *The Glass Menagerie,* in which a lame, withdrawn girl blossoms under the attentions of her "gentleman caller" who turns out to be brought along by her brother simply out of pity and to still his mother's nagging. This sad and charming play is overshadowed by such powerful slabs of sexuality and violence as *A Streetcar Named Desire* and *Cat on a Hot Tin Roof.* The former is the better, with its clash between a fragile, genteel woman and a virile apelike man, ending in rape and madness.

Arthur Miller is probably a far more solid and worthwhile playwright. Themes: betrayal and the need for a "clean name" in society. They appear first in *All My Sons,* about a war profiteer whose past erupts to shatter the present, and *Death of a Salesman,* in which a modern Everyman, who is neurotically obsessed by "success," betrays and ruins his sons' chances in life.

You, as a bluffer, should hail this as a modern tragic masterpiece, although you can privately think *The Crucible* Miller's best play. Written after his experiences with McCarthyism, it is a study in mass hysteria based on the seventeeth-century affair of the witches of Salem. *A View from the Bridge,* set in New York's waterfront, is concerned with another tragic obsession, a man's intense love for his niece.

This section ends with a couple of Swiss, Max Frisch and Friedrich Dürrenmatt. The latter is more popular with the public, the former with intellectuals.

Frisch's *The Fire Raisers* was first a failure, but it was not long before its reputation began to soar: nothing, after all, is more helpful to a cult play than a resounding flop. The trappings of *The Fire Raisers* are of the old expressionist type, and the plot follows the mounting panic of a bourgeois businessman who, despite a scare about arson in the district, gives lodging to two strange men. Like a frightened rabbit, he is hypnotized by their bravado and brutality as they fill his attic with drums of gasoline. Finally he lends them a box of matches, and the curtain falls on the house and town in flames. A postscript set in heaven provides justification for the businessman, as the fire has helped in the city's rebuilding plans. The parallel with the rise of Nazism, appeasement, and German's prosperity after the war are obvious, but in spite of heavy symbolism *The Fire Raisers* has genuine power. Somehow though, it lacks humanity, and the same applies, rather oddly in view of its subject, to Frisch's later play *Andorra,* about a man persecuted because he is supposed to be a Jew.

Dürrenmatt, however, has had more popular acclaim, particularly with *The Physicists,* in which three scientists retire to a mental home in the hope of preserving their discoveries, and recently in *Meteor* and *The Visit.* As with Frisch, Dürrenmatt's plays smack of modern morality plays somewhat in the German tradition of forty years ago.

BERTOLT BRECHT

THE CULT OF BRECHT, to which the bluffer should piously bow, is a really fascinating one, for its produces violent passions both for and against. Up to 1949, when Brecht had nearly all his important work behind him, many theatre commentators dismissed him as a follower of the expressionists, Toller and Kaiser; a Marxist who wrote rather clumsy and obvious symbolic plays, one of which, *The Threepenny Opera,* was notable for its music and for having been "borrowed" from *The Beggar's Opera.*

The story is curiously sad and even farcical. Brecht, who wanted most of all to influence and instruct the masses, succeeded only in setting intellectuals aflame. The man whose avowed creed as a director and theorist was, by means of the *"V-Effekt"* (Alienation Effect, see below), to dispel illusionistic hocus-pocus in the theatre and replace emotional identification of the audience with characters on the stage by intellectual appreciation of the story, wrote plays like *Mother Courage* which involved the spectator immediately. Such contradictions are fine fare for the bluffer, who should be ready to uphold Brecht as a flawed genius.

One thing must be said right away: Brecht's plays are far from being Germanic and dull (with certain appalling exceptions). At

their best they are hard, muscular, and direct with no naturalistic
fripperies. The recurring subject matter of decadence, greed, exploitation, and slum values has generally, of course, enormous appeal
to the intellectual; Brecht's didactic works, which are concerned with
the honest strivings of the proletariat, are not nearly as interesting.
Nevertheless, the bluffer *must* read the main plays, and he should
certainly say that he has seen incomparable productions of them by
the Berliner Ensemble, Brecht's own East Berlin company.

You need not bother much with Brecht's earliest plays (although
you should certainly know of them), including *Baal* and *Mann ist
Mann*. They date from 1915 to the mid-twenties and are in the
fashionable expressionistic style of the German theatre of the time,
and are largely overdone protests against corruption and decadence.
Note that already a typical Brechtian paradox is appearing; while
expressly antiromantic, the plays use all the wild action and larger-
than-life characters of romantic theatre to press home their point.

In 1928 came Brecht's most popular and most immediately
enjoyable play. *The Threepenny Opera* is in the ballad-opera style
of its original, John Gay's *The Beggar's Opera* of the early eighteenth
century, with tart, nostalgic, German cabaret jazz accompaniments
by Kurt Weill. It even provided a hit number for the Top Ten in
"The Ballad of Mack the Knife."

Set in late-Victorian London, the *Opera* presents the familiar
tale of Mackie Messer or Mack the Knife, who marries Polly Pea-
chum, the daughter of a fence and leader of a gang of professional
beggars, and is betrayed to the authorities by his other women. The
criminals of the play are good bourgeois citizens with normal middle-
class tastes and morality: the "wickedness" of the professionals is
nothing to what goes on in respectable society—after all, "What is
robbing a bank compared to founding a bank?" The sick, sour humor
of the play catches exactly the cynicism and disgust of the late
twenties, and indeed, of this century.

Two other "musicals" of this time are *Happy End*, involving
Chicago crooks and a Salvation Army girl, and *The Rise and Fall
of the City of Mahagonny*. This town is founded by crooks so that
they can work in real freedom, but it becomes too respectable until
an approaching hurricane introduces a policy of do-what-you-like
and the city riots itself to pieces.

Now in the thirties comes Brecht's Marxist period, but he could never toe the party line for very long. You can safely pass over the worthy, rather dreary plays of this time, when Brecht was in Scandinavia where he had fled from the Nazis. You should note, however, *St. Joan of the Stockyards* (Brecht had a thing about Joan of Arc), another play about commercial exploitation in Chicago. Again, his ideas of Chicago are about as odd as his conception of London in *The Threepenny Opera*.

In the late thirties began the series of plays on which Brecht's reputation really rests: *Life of Galileo, Mother Courage and Her Children, The Good Woman* (or *Person,* depending on the translation) *of Setzuan, Herr Puntila and His Man Matti, The Resistible Rise of Arturo Ui, Schweyk in the Second World War,* and *The Caucasian Chalk Circle.* In the middle of this output Brecht fled to America when the Nazis overran Norway. He returned to Germany in 1949 to run the Berliner Ensemble in East Berlin, writing nothing more of note for the stage. He died in 1956. The Ensemble, led by his wife, Helene Weigel, carries on his ideas and a repertoire of his plays.

There is not room here to summarize Brecht's important plays from *Galileo* to *The Caucasian Chalk Circle,* but a number of themes recur, and the bluffer should conscientiously note them:

1. The poor are *basically* good in their earthy vulgarity; the rich are inevitably corrupt and decadent;

2. Goodness in this criminal world is suicidal: to exist, man has always to compromise, at the very least accepting expedients, and to succeed he must outcheat the rest;

3. Each person has two sides, good and evil.

The vigor and variety of Brecht at his best is seen in *Mother Courage,* the story of a tough old canteen woman whose livelihood consists in trailing after the mercenary armies of the Thirty Years' War. She loses her children but still clings with materialistic devotion to her job, in spite of all the tragedy it has cost her, because it is the only way of life she knows. Of all Brecht's plays this is perhaps the most deeply felt: it is definitely the most moving. The "Brechtian" trappings of songs embedded in the action, simple rudimentary staging and placards or projected texts to set the scene are all there, but they are transcended by the power and humor of the writing.

Another example of the main themes effectively presented is *The Good Woman of Setzuan,* in which Shen Te, a warmhearted prostitute, is forced to disguise herself as her (imaginary) ruthless male cousin in order to survive.

The good bluffer will use the word "Brechtian" a lot. It applies not so much to his plays but to Brecht's theories and methods of production. First of all we must get the Alienation Effect clear. Quote it in German if your accent is good enough: *Verfremdungs-effekt.* It does not mean alienating the audience. Brecht rebeled against both romanticism and naturalism, and the intention of the Effect is to set everything on the stage in a new and unfamiliar light. To do this, the director should encourage the spectator to enjoy with the mind, rather than be taken in by cheap illusion and emotion. He must be constantly reminded that he is in a theatre and he must be critical. Staging, therefore, must never outdo reality, and the actors must remain at a distance from the characters they are playing, taking an obvious attitude to these characters. This is in direct opposition to the Stanislavski and Method schools of acting.

"Brechtian" at its cheapest level means plays with bare, uncompromising staging with songs during the action and often a general air of earnest gloom—you will find that newspaper critics apply it indiscriminately to any recent play of even slightly unconventional form.

A somewhat earlier theory of Brecht's, but leading to the Alienation Effect, is the idea of *Epic Theatre,* a phrase you should find useful. It belongs to the twenties and means, as you have probably already guessed, a style of production that is directed at the audience's reason instead of the emotions. It has nothing whatever to do with Cecil B. de Mille, but precisely the opposite: it is argument, generally political, presented in bare, spare fashion and the spectator has to be convinced, not swept off his feet by feelings.

Brecht's disciples have followed Brecht's dictums far more closely than the master could himself. He was a theatre man through and through, and as much as he fought against the old glamour of the stage he could not avoid it, and his best plays will always be those with tough, earthy characters, intensely human, that immediately catch an audience's sympathy.

There are many admirers of the great man; there are many who hate his guts.

THE "THEATRES"—OF CRUELTY, THE ABSURD, AND FACT

THESE ARE HANDY, RATHER vague terms, but be careful not to apply them to the wrong playwrights and directors. However absurd you think Brecht, say, he is definitely not Absurd. The first two, the Theatres of Cruelty and the Absurd, can be bracketed to some extent as the Theatre of the Sick. The Theatre of Fact, however, is very different indeed and harks back to the political, didactic theatre of the thirties.

The Theatre of Cruelty is director's rather than dramatist's theatre, in which the author's text is only a starting point in an effort to liberate the audience's subconscious, to bring out those repressions that are usually safely locked up in order to make the audience react and sit up. Naturally, as these involve the nastier aspects of human nature, the Theatre of Cruelty puts on the stage the extremes of madness, torture, and perversion. These aspects are generally set in an atmosphere of ritual, fantasy, and magic; reason and logic are anathema.

Cruelty is far from new on the stage. The ancient Greeks gorily removed Oedipus's eyes, Shakespeare did the same for Gloucester in *King Lear,* and the number of ingenious deaths and tortures in Elizabethan and Jacobean plays must rival the number of Indians who bite the dust in Westerns. All the same, it took the twentieth century to turn cruelty into a theatrical movement of its own.

The important name in the T. of C. is Antonin Artaud, a surrealistic Frenchman who founded in the mid-thirties his own Théâtre de la Cruauté. The dedicated bluffer should try to read Artaud's theories in *The Theater and Its Double,* for its influence and inspiration for Peter Brook. This British director made an astonishingly Cruel foray in his famous production of *The Persecution and Assassination of Marat as Performed by the Inmates of the Asylum of Charenton Under the Direction of the Marquis de Sade* (usually known, affectionately, as the *Marat/Sade*), written by Peter Weiss. In this graphic and exact representation of lunacy, the minutiae of madness were exploited to the full. You must not, at the moment, be the slightest bit critical of this particular *tour de force*—but be ready to attack as soon as theatrical fashion changes.

This theatrical horror-comic movement is, in a curious way, rather romantic, and you will notice, and say, how violently opposed this is to Brecht's theories of a theatre appealing to reason, not the emotions. A neat and useful phrase for the all-out assault on the senses that characterizes the T. of C. in the Artaud style is *total theatre*.

There is only one major dramatist of the T. of C. and he is claimed partly by the Theatre of the Absurd. He is Jean Genet.

Most little boys grow up with ambitions to be locomotive engineers, pilots, doctors, or policemen. Not so Genet: he wanted to be a thief. He did not find it difficult to achieve this wish, and he added to it by becoming a homosexual and, while in prison in occupied France, a poet. You should know of three plays by Genet: *The Maids*, *The Balcony*, and *The Blacks*. Ritual and fantasy are strong in all of them.

The Maids is about two sisters united in hatred who resolve to kill their young and lovely mistress. They are in the habit of working out their fantasies by acting the parts of mistress and servant, and when their murder attempt fails, they continue this game and one maid poisons the other. Genet originally required the three women's parts in *The Maids* to be played by young men, and the key to understanding the play lies in the envy the underlings have for the attractive life of their social superiors, whom they ape ritually.

Ritual occurs again in *The Balcony*. The regulars of Madame Irma's brothel express their fantasies by dressing up and acting the parts of bishops, judges, or generals. When revolution comes to their country, Madame Irma's customers take up real-life roles as bishop, judge, and general with a plumber as chief of police. Wish-fulfillment in the realms of sex and power are once more a main theme.

The Blacks has no plot; Negroes act out their resentment against white domination, and a high spot of the play is the ritual murder, performed in loving detail, of a white woman. The blacks are a symbol for the outcasts of society. The play had considerable success in Paris and New York but baffled most of those who saw it.

Genet's intention is to shock the audience, by means of scenes of degradation onstage, into a realization that their own fantasies are identical with those of society's dregs.

The Theatre of the Absurd seems to be largely based on the hopeful maxim that human life has no purpose: man is born to be frustrated and out of key with the universe. Nothing is rational or logical in real life, so the keynote of the Theatre of the Absurd is tragic farce.

The plays tend to be set on rubbish dumps, in automobile junk-yards, tottering tenements, and other locations with potent symbolism for the twentieth century. Although most of the exponents of this cheerful philosophy live in Paris, not all of them are French. It all began, however, with the Frenchman Alfred Jarry (who ended up appropriately enough in an asylum), someone whom we shall hear much more of in the next few years.

Jarry wrote a play called *Ubu Roi* (*King Ubu*), and its first night in 1896 caused a glorious scandal in Paris. To begin with, the first word spoken was the expletive "Merde!"—which had the effect of a depth charge, rather as though an actor had come through the curtains of a New York theatre of the period and shouted "Shit!" at the audience. Not surprisingly, it was a quarter of an hour before the uproar subsided enough for the performance to continue, and from them on the evening was stormy, to say the least.

Ubu, Jarry's "hero," is the personification of ugly, Rabelaisian bourgeois greed and cowardice. As King of Poland he attacks Russia, murders and swindles, but is beaten in the end. The actors performed rather like puppets and the scenery was derived from children's draw-ings. Other Ubu plays followed: *Ubu Enchaîné* and *Ubu Cocu,* and Jarry was also the founder of a zany philosophy, pataphysics, the "science of imaginary solutions." It is wildly serious, wildly farcial, and the bluffer should get to know something about this particular brand of deliberate nonsense.

The Theatre of the Absurd was off with a bang, although it did not achieve its name until the fifties. The next manifestations were a surrealist squib by the poet Guillaume Apollinaire in 1917, *Les Mamelles de Tirésias* (The Breasts of Tiresias), and various bits and pieces by the Dadaists. A particular failing of the genre, incidentally, is the difficulty Absurd dramatists have found in sustaining full-length plays. Brecht flirted with the Absurd, notably in *Mann ist Mann,* but the next important name is the director Antonin Artaud, whom we have already met in the Theatre of Cruelty: his style of production was influenced by both Balinese dancing and the Marx Brothers. Artaud's assistants included Jean-Louis Barrault, later famous as actor and director, and Roger Blin, who became the leading Absurdist director in France.

The Absurd hit New York in 1956 with the brilliant staging by Herbert Berghof of *Waiting for Godot* by Samuel Beckett, an Irish novelist writing in French and living in Paris. The play in which "Nothing happens, nobody goes, it's awful" presents two decrepit tramps (there are so many in current drama that it might be called the Theatre of the Bum), Vladimir and Estragon, waiting by the roadside for someone who will alter their lives, Godot, to turn up. He never does, but two other characters appear from time to time, master and servant, Pozzo and Lucky. Yearning and futility are two of the themes, but you can read all sorts of messages into *Godot,* and that, no doubt, is partly the reason for its enormous success. It is without question one of the most important works of twentieth-century drama, and the bluffer should not only know it, he should also be able to quote from it.

Beckett's next essay in the Absurd was *Endgame,* the dustbin play. Hamn, blind and ancient, and his servant Clov (note the parallel with Pozzo and Lucky in *Godot*) with Hamm's legless parents, Nagg and Nell, in ashcans, are going to leave the room in which they are the sole survivors of some unspecified world catastrophe. The characters hate one another and are on the point of departing forever. They don't.

The bluffer should also know of, and perhaps even read, *Krapp's Last Tape, Happy Days* (in which the heroine ends up being buried up to her neck), and *Play* (which has three characters with their heads sticking out of urns. In performance, the actors go through the text twice).

Not as widely known other than as a name, and therefore good bluff material, is Arthur Adamov. Of his work you should pretend knowledge of *Ping Pong* (use the original French title, *Le Ping-Pong*), a lesson in the danger of falling victim of illusion. Futility, it goes without saying, is also a theme. A medical student and an art student play through their life at a pinball machine, becoming more and more at its mercy, until one of them drops dead. Adamov, by birth a Russian, now living in Paris, is a Marxist, and his later plays have become political rather than simply Absurd.

Now a really big fish. Eugène Ionesco also lives in Paris but comes from Romania. Like many Absurd writers, he is at his best with short pieces, and his first, *The Bald Soprano,* is, you should remember, of dazzling brilliance. The difficulty of communication between people is an Ionesco theme, "the tragedy of language." It all began when Ionesco started to learn English, and found that the dialogue of his conversation primer, largely the cliché and truism of characters busily telling each other what they already know, made him dizzy. Thus, *The Bald Soprano,* acted with deadly seriousness as an "antiplay," on its first night was a dead flop. Undeterred, Ionesco continued writing.

His second play, *The Lesson,* in which the teacher rapes his pupil, is also concerned mainly with language. A vital work in the Ionesco canon is *The Chairs.* In this, two old people attempt to pass on a message to posterity, and employ an orator to do so. The stage becomes crowded with an imaginary audience, and assured that the orator will now communicate the message, the couple jump out the window. The orator can produce nothing but a meaningless jumble of sounds and letters on a blackboard. A great many Absurd ideas come together here, and Ionesco himself says helpfully that the theme is "nothingness."

These plays, and several others, are all short. *Amedée, or How to Get Rid of It* is full-length. A writer, who after years of effort has produced only two lines of a play, and his wife live in a room from which they have not moved for fifteen years. In the next room is a corpse. It grows bigger and bigger and toadstools flourish on the stage; eventually a gigantic foot smashes into the couple's room. The body represents their dead love, now poisoning their lives. Amedée, the husband, manages to push the corpse out of the window, and in the last act it floats away with him like a balloon. This, you will be relieved to hear, is a hopeful play for once, showing the necessity of striking out for a new life.

Tueur sans gages (The Killer) is about the inevitability of death. Bérenger, the little Chaplin-like hero, is introduced to a Utopian town, the radiant city where even permanent sunshine is built in. To his horror, Bérenger learns that a merciless killer is abroad in this paradise, and the play follows his search for this character and his eventual discovery. At the end is an immensely long speech in which he pleads with the killer, who remains silent except for a quiet giggle, but finally and willingly, Bérenger succumbs to the knife. The moral is, roughly, that human life can be only fitfully happy, that behind every silver lining is a dirty great cloud.

Bérenger appears again in *Rhinoceros,* as the only man to stand out against a monstrous attack of rhinoceritis that is infecting every person in his town, turning them into rhinos. The theme, very obviously, is the fatal lure of brute political movements like fascism, but Bérenger is also seen as a ridiculous individual who makes a virtue of futile individuality.

Ionesco is a magic name for the bluffer; he is a playwright of astonishing brilliance who is likely to outlive mere fashionable success. Note, however, that some intellectuals don't love him.

Such are the major dramatists of the Absurd, but there are many others, minor and major, whose work contains Absurd elements. It may be useful to note the following names.

Jean Tardieu, the poet, has written little more than sketches for the stage, but they are numerous and anticipate Ionesco in their subject matter, but are even more experimental and surrealistic.

Boris Vian is best known for his one Absurd play, *The Empire Builders,* which introduces a family trying to escape in their own house from a peculiar and terrifying noise that chases them from room to room. One of the characters is a silent subhuman, the *schmurtz,* constantly kicked and battered by the others. In the end the peculiar *schmurtz* dies, but an army of other *schmurtzes* replaces him. The symbolism of the noise is clear—death—but no one has yet explained the scapegoat *schmurtz* satisfactorily.

Fernando Arrabal is a Spaniard writing in French of whom we shall hear more—so take note. His plays have a somewhat frightening mixture of childishness and cruelty, and he is an acknowledged disciple of Beckett. Of his several plays in which he seems to say that goodness is utterly futile, *Le Cimetière des voitures* (*The Automobile Graveyard*) is his most accomplished. It is both blasphemous and innocent, the passion of Christ played out by people living among the corpses of cars. Arrabal has also flirted with abstract theatre that consists of the mechanical movements of three-dimensional shapes. His latest play is *And They Put Handcuffs on the Flowers.*

Dino Buzzatti, the Italian novelist, has written one important Absurd play, *Un Caso Clinico* (*A Clinical Case*). It has a curious affinity with Vian's *The Empire Builders* in its theme of the approach of death. A rich businessman goes into a strange clinic for observation on the top floor. Gradually, he is transferred downward, floor by floor, among cases who are progressively more seriously ill. He ends up on the ground floor where every patient dies. The prosperous man is reduced by life and the bureaucracy around him to utter degradation, in the style of a morality play.

America has produced two playwrights in the style, Edward Albee and Arthur L. Kopit. Albee's plays, *Zoo Story* and *The American Dream*, attack comfortable American ideals and commercial habits. The latter makes great fun of cliché and homey sentimentality in presenting the perfect American male: healthy, keen, but devoid of soul. His best-known play is *Who's Afraid of Virginia Woolf?* But in this he departs from the Absurd to comedy of manners *cum* domestic drama. A picture of American campus life, of two couples tearing each other to pieces, it is nevertheless very good theatre, and the bluffer will praise it, if only for its title.

Arthur L. Kopit is notable for having won second prize for the longest title in modern drama with *Oh Dad, Poor Dad, Momma's Hung You in the Closet and I'm Feeling So Sad* (the first prize, of course, is held by *Marat/Sade*), and that for the shortest title, by The Royal Shakespeare Company with *US*. One great sick, tragic joke, *Oh Dad* is a Freudian fantasy about a young man and his dragon of a dominating mother who travels everywhere with her husband who is dead, stuffed and in a coffin. Kopit's other play, *Indians*, failed on Broadway.

The Theatre of Fact is simply documentary theatre. As is the case with most up-to-the-minute theatrical movements, its roots lie some time back. In this case, the American social-consciousness theatre of the thirties can be said to have started it all, with the presentation of actual events in the *Living Newspaper* productions. The Theatre of Fact offers an interpretation of real happenings by re-creating them —as far as possible on the stage—either verbatim, using actual recorded speeches, or in fictionalized reconstructions.

A few years ago Rolf Hochhuth, an intense young German dramatist, cause riots all over Europe for daring to attack Pope Pius XII for his alleged failure to speak out against Hitler's persecution of the Jews. *The Deputy* is a great chunk of debate dressed up with classy contemporary production, but it blazed the trail for the political playwrights of 1966 and 1967.

Hochhuth's other play is *The Soldiers,* with its theme of the moral responsibility of those who ordered the mass bombing of Germany.

A colorful example of the Theatre of Fact was the Royal Shakespeare Company's *US* (you can make of the title what you will: it can mean both "us" and U.S.—United States), a highly theatrical essay on the war in Vietnam. The front row of the audience found that they were inclined to participate in this experience a little too much when actors with paper bags over their heads, representing the dumb masses of Vietnam, fell over their (the audience's) legs. Animal lovers got hot under the collar because a butterfly appeared to suffer immolation on stage. At the end of the evening, the cast remained staring stonily at the audience, daring it to leave the theatre. In fact, a high old time was had by everyone concerned with the production. It was an all-out assault on the senses and the mind in the style of "total theatre" after the prophet Artaud.

A much quieter example of the Theatre of Fact was *In the Matter of J. Robert Oppenheimer* by Heinar Kipphardt. This was selected material from transcripts made at the Congressional investigation into the loyalty of nuclear scientist Oppenheimer, who had been instrumental in producing the first atom bomb but who got cold moral feet about going on with the infinitely more destructive hydrogen bomb. The whole effect is unsatisfying compared to a work of imagination.

It is not clear which way the Theatre of Fact will develop: in the all-out, emotive, sweep-em-off-their-feet style of *US,* or the sober presentation of unalterable fact of *In the Matter of J. Robert Oppenheimer*. Anyway, the ambitious bluffer should follow the next moves with passionate interest.

IN AMERICA

TO BLUFF SUCCESSFULLY IN THE theatre, certain basic bits of information must be dredged up and disseminated at proper intervals so that the bluffer appears equally equipped to pontificate upon the threatre's past, present, and future. In this section, we will, therefore, be supplying names of directors, producers, actors, designers, composers, lyricists, choreographers, and so on, who have added to the luster of the American theatre, since the previous chapters have dealt with the major theatrical movements in Europe at some length. We will include pertinent facts regarding some of the more interesting aspects of Off-Broadway, Off-Off-Broadway; touch on stock theatre, regional theatre, and repertory theatre, and offer other tidbits that help make the theatre such a rich source of fascination to the so-called "civilians."

Let us consider some of this lore.

OUT OF THE PAST

American theatre goes back to the early 1800s (who can forget Mr. Lincoln's theatre party?) but its Golden Era commenced around the late 1880s and is either still going on, or it ended in 19___ (supply your own year).

Be that as it may, the following were among the luminaries who set Broadway aflame in the gaslight era. It pays to commit their names to memory since it immediately establishes you as a serious student of the theatre. In the parentheses, we will list the stars' most famous role or roles for additional bluffing impact:

Edwin Booth (*Hamlet*) He was, of course, the brother of John Wilkes Booth, the pioneer of the popular American sport of assassinating public figures.

Edwin Forrest (*Metamora*) Supporters of this gentleman once started a riot that killed over twenty people.

Adah Isaacs Menken (*Mazeppa*) The nation's first glamour girl.

Joe Jefferson III (*Rip Van Winkle*)
Lotta Crabtree (*Little Nell*)
John Drew (Various roles) John Barrymore's uncle.
Richard Mansfield (*Dr. Jekyll and Mr. Hyde*)
James O'Neill (*The Count of Monte Cristo*) Eugene's pappy.
Minnie Maddern Fiske (*Becky Sharp*)
William Gillette (*Sherlock Holmes*)
Maude Adams (*Peter Pan*)
Julia Marlowe and E. H. Sothern (*Macbeth*)
Sarah Bernhardt (*The Lady of the Camillias*) Miss Bernhardt is to
    be remembered for her wooden leg and her iron will. Sarah was
    one of the first women to essay the title role in Hamlet.
Helena Modjeska (Beatrice in *Much Ado About Nothing*)

Latter-day stars included:

Ethel Barrymore (*The Constant Wife*) She scored her first triumph
    in *Captain Jinks of the Horse Marines*.
John Barrymore (*Hamlet*)
Lionel Barrymore (*Peter Ibbetson*)
Laurette Taylor (*Peg o' My Heart*) She later made a big hit as the
    mother in *The Glass Menagerie*.
Otis Skinner (*The Taming of the Shrew*) Cornelia's father.
Frank Bacon (*Lightnin'*)
Eleanora Duse (*The Lady of the Camillias*)

Some early theatre entrepreneurs were:

Charles and Daniel Frohman
David Belasco (He always wore a priest's collar)
Steele Mackaye (the Mike Todd of his day)
William A. Brady

Early playwrights were:

Clyde Fitch (*Beau Brummel, The Truth, The City, Captain Jinks
    of the Horse Marines, The Climbers, Barbara Frietchie, Her
    Own Way*)
James Barrie (*Peter Pan, The Admirable Crichton, Little Mary*)

The Incomparable G. B. Shaw (*Arms and the Man, The Devil's Disciple, Man and Superman, Mrs. Warren's Profession, Androcles and the Lion,* etc., etc., etc.)

Arthur Wing Pinero (*The Profligate, The Second Mrs. Tanqueray*)

Edward Sheldon (*The Nigger, Salvation Nell, The Jest, Romance*)

Owen Davis (*Nellie the Beautiful Cloak Model, Ethan Frome*)

Eugene Watter (*Paid in Full, The Easiest Way*—both real shockers of the day).

MUSICAL COMEDY

The first stupendous musical hit in the American theatre was *The Black Crook.* The next was *The Little Tycoon,* and finally, *Florodora,* which gave birth to the famous Florodora Sextette, six fetching ladies who set male hearts afire and created a nationwide sensation.

Other musical hits of the earlier days were Victor Herbert's *Babes in Toyland, Naughty Marietta,* and *The Red Mill;* Florenz Ziegfeld's annual Follies; George M. Cohan's *Little Johnny Jones, Forty-Five Minutes from Broadway.*

COMPOSERS

Some early composers on Broadway were:

Rudolf Friml (*The Firefly, Rose Marie, The Vagabond King, The Three Musketeers*)

Sigmund Romberg (*Maytime, The Desert Song, The Student Prince, Blossom Time*)

Jerome Kern (*Showboat, Roberta, Sally, Very Warm for May, Sunny, Music in the Air*)

George Gershwin (*Strike Up the Band, Of Thee I Sing, Porgy and Bess, Let Them Eat Cake, Lady Be Good, Girl Crazy*)

Other significant composers have been:

Cole Porter (*The Gay Divorce, Anything Goes, Kiss Me Kate, Leave It to Me, Du Barry Was a Lady, Panama Hattie, Let's Face It,*

Something for the Boys, Mexican Hayride, Can-Can, Silk Stockings)

Irving Berlin (*As Thousands Cheer, Call Me Madam, Face the Music, Louisiana Purchase, Annie Get Your Gun, Miss Liberty*)

Kurt Weill (*Street Scene, Lost in the Stars, Love Life, Lady in the Dark, Knickerbocker Holiday*)

Richard Rodgers (*On Your Toes, Babes in Arms, I Married an Angel, The Boys from Syracuse, I'd Rather Be Right, Pal Joey, Oklahoma!, Carousel, No Strings, Allegro, The King and I, South Pacific, The Sound of Music, Pipe Dream, Me and Juliet.*

Frank Loesser (*Guys and Dolls, Where's Charley?, The Most Happy Fella, How to Succeed in Business Without Really Trying*)

Leonard Bernstein (*On the Town, Wonderful Town, Candide, West Side Story*)

Frederic Loewe (*My Fair Lady, Brigadoon, Paint Your Wagon, Camelot*)

Richard Adler and Jerry Ross (*Pajama Game, Damn Yankees*)

Harold Arlen (*Bloomer Girl, Jamaica, St. Louis Woman, House of Flowers*)

Harold Rome (*Pins and Needles, Call Me Mister, Wish You Were Here, Destry Rides Again, I Can Get It For You Wholesale, Fanny, Gone With the Wind*)

Arthur Schwartz (*The Little Show, Three's a Crowd, The Bandwagon, Inside U.S.A., A Tree Grows in Brooklyn, By the Beautiful Sea*)

Jule Styne (*High Button Shoes, Gentlemen Prefer Blondes, Bells Are Ringing, Gypsy, Two on the Aisle, Funny Girl, Sugar*)

Jerry Bock (*Fiddler on the Roof, Mr. Wonderful, The Apple Tree, Fiorello!, Tenderloin*)

Jerry Herman (*Dolly, Mame, Milk and Honey*)

Mitch Leigh (*Man of La Mancha*)

Burton Lane (*Finian's Rainbow, On a Clear Day You Can See Forever*)

Bob Merrill (*Carnival; Henry, Sweet Henry; New Girl in Town, Take Me Along*)

John Kander (*Cabaret, The Happy Time, Flora the Red Menace*)

Cy Coleman (*Sweet Charity*)

Charles Strouse (*Bye Bye Birdie, Golden Boy*)

Meredith Willson (*The Music Man, The Unsinkable Molly Brown*)
Harvey Schmidt (*The Fantasticks, 110 in the Shade, I Do! I Do!*)
And of course, George M. Cohan.

Other important composers for the American musical stage were Vincent Youmans (*No, No, Nanette, Hit the Deck*); Gian-Carlo Menotti (*The Medium, The Consul, The Saint of Bleecker Street*), and Marc Blitzstein (*The Cradle Will Rock, No for an Answer, Regina*).

Harry Ruby contributed music for musicals as did Sammy Fain, J. Fred Coots, Vernon Duke, Jimmy McHugh, and Harry Tierney. Some latter-day names are Lionel Bart (*Oliver*) and Anthony Newley (*Stop the World—I Want to Get Off; The Roar of the Greasepaint— The Smell of the Crowd*); Melvin Van Peebles (*Ain't Supposed to Die a Natural Death, Don't Play Us Cheap*); Galt MacDermott (*Hair, Two Gentlemen of Verona*).

LYRICISTS

Noted lyricists of past and present include:

Lorenz Hart who teamed with Richard Rodgers and Oscar Hammerstein II

Betty Comden and Adolf Green (*On the Town, Wonderful Town, Two on the Aisle, Bells Are Ringing*)

Ira Gershwin (*Lady Be Good, Lady in the Dark, Porgy and Bess, Of Thee I Sing*)

Alan Jay Lerner (*My Fair Lady, Camelot, What's Up?, The Day Before Spring, Brigadoon, Paint Your Wagon, On a Clear Day You Can See Forever*)

Stephen Sondheim (*West Side Story, Gypsy, Follies, Anyone Can Whistle, Do I Hear a Waltz?, Company*—Sondheim is also a most talented composer)

Sheldon Harnick (he collaborates with Jerry Bock)

E.Y. (Yip) Harburg (*Finian's Rainbow, Dorothy and the Wizard of Oz,* etc.)

Dorothy Fields

John La Touche

Howard Dietz (teamed with Arthur Schwartz)

Sammy Cahn
E. Ray Goetz
Irving Caesar
Johnny Mercer
Fred Ebb
Lee Adams
Buddy de Sylva
Tom Jones
Carolyn Leigh

Also, many of the aforementioned composers wrote their own lyrics (Porter, Berlin, Loesser, etc.).

CHOREOGRAPHERS

Well-known choreographers on Broadway are or have been:

Agnes de Mille   Jack Cole
Jerome Robbins   Helen Tamiris
Bob Fosse   Robert Alton
Ron Field   Michael Kidd
George Ballanchine   Onna White
Gower Champion   Peter Gennaro
Hanya Holm

MUSICAL DIRECTORS

Successful musical directors have included:

George Abbott   George S. Kaufman
Harold Prince   Bob Fosse
Joe Layton   Albert Marro
Moss Hart   Joe Anthony
Joshua Logan   Rouben Mamoulian
Hassard Short   Tom O'Horgan
Gower Champion   Peter Coe
Jerome Robbins   Herb Ross
Abe Burrows

LIBRETTISTS

Well-known librettists (book writers) have been and are:

Arthur Laurents (*West Side Story, Company, Gypsy*)
Comden and Green
James Goldman (*Follies*)
Joe Stein (*Fiddler, Zorba*)
Neil Simon (more about him later)
Alan Jay Lerner
Oscar Hammerstein
Michael Stewart
Abe Burrows
Herbert Fields, Dorothy Fields, and Joseph Fields
George Abbott (again)

Josh Logan
Howard Lindsay and Russel Crouse
Guy Bolton
E.Y. (Yip) Harburg
Otto Harbach
Moss Hart
Laurence Schwab
George S. Kaufman
Morrie Ryskind
N. Richard Nash
Peter Stone (*1776, Skyscraper, Sugar*)

STARS AND SEMISTARS

Some of the more popular musical stars on Broadway have been:

George M. Cohan
Elsie Janis
Eddie Foy
Lillian Russell
Fanny Brice
Jimmy Durante
Ed Wynn
Eddie Cantor
Al Jolson
Marilyn Miller
William Gaxton
Joe Cook
Victor Moore
Ethel Waters
Fred Stone
Gertrude Niesen

Bert Lahr
Bea Lillie
Ann Pennington
W. C. Fields
Fred and Adele Astaire
Gertrude Lawrence
Willie and Eugene Howard
Ina Claire
Will Rogers
Helen Morgan
Ray Middleton
Olsen and Johnson
Ella Logan
Ray Bolger
Sophie Tucker
Danny Kaye

Alfred Drake
Jimmy Savo
June Havoc
Vivienne Segal
Ronny Graham
Celeste Holm
Howard da Silva

Howard Keel
John Raitt
Gwen Verdon
Mary Martin, and the incomparable
Ethel Merman

Other well-known musical performers have been:

Betty Garrett
Walter Slezak
Patsy Kelly
Helen Kane
Clifton Webb
Helen Broderick
Jack Haley
Shirley Booth
Nanette Fabray
Robert Preston
Cyril Ritchard
Phil Silvers
Carol Haney
Jack Whiting

Doretta Morrow
Monty Woolley
Tamara
Kate Smith
Charles Winninger
Charles Ruggles
Mitzi Green
The Marx Brothers
Ruth Etting
Wilbur Evans
Helen Gallagher
Allyn McLerie
Joan McCracken
Irene Bordoni

and more recently—

Carol Channing
Julie Andrews
Zero Mostel

Angela Lansbury
Robert Morse
Richard Kiley

The alert theatre bluffer will frequently announce that *Oklahoma!* changed the American musical picture, and that *Hair* represented the next revolutionary phase.

DRAMA

Once the mainstay of the American theatre, there is little room for drama on the Broadway stage—these days it is mainly confined to the university and the experimental theatres. The reason—as given by the so-called experts—is that people will not shell out eight dollars to watch serious theatre, but will pay up to fifteen dollars to watch grimy, naked children somnambulate through such musical extravaganzas as *Hair, Jesus Christ Superstar, Grease, Godspell,* or *Two Gentlemen of Verona.*

Until the beginning of the 1920s, Broadway dramas ran almost exclusively to the *East Lynne* mold: the stalwart hero, the pure heroine, the scenery-chewing villian, the kindhearted grandfather. Then, several things happened. One was the war that banished American's innocence forever. Another was the emergence of muckraking American novelists, critics, and opinion molders who felt the time ripe for a more mature approach in the arts. A third was Eugene O'Neill.

Mr. O'Neill, a tortured and highly introspective personality, began to write plays that grated on the American conscience and made theatregoers sit up and listen to the turgid words and passions being declaimed before them. He wrote about the sea in symbolic terms derivative of Herman Melville; he plumbed the depths of human emotion and laid bare a fabric of national existence heretofore largely unexplored on the American stage.

Beginning with his three one-acters about the sea produced by the Provincetown Players, he followed with play after play to establish himself as the foremost dramatist of the American theatre, a position he still maintains despite powerful challenges by Messers. Miller and Williams.

O'Neill, whose father, the mercurial James, was one of the nation's foremost stage idols of his day, was a prodigious worker. Between bouts of drinking, illness, melancholia, and general cussedness, he managed to turn out such memorable dramas as: *Beyond the Horizon, Anna Christie* (later, the musical, *New Girl In Town*), *All God's Chillun Got Wings, Desire Under the Elms, The Great God Brown, The Hairy Ape, Mourning Becomes Electra, Strange Interlude, Emperor Jones, Marco Millions; Ah, Wilderness!* (in which George M. Cohan played a leading role), *The Iceman Cometh, A Moon for the Misbegotten, Long Day's Journey Into Night, More Stately Mansions,* and many, many more. He left a mark on the Broadway theatre that, most authorities agree, will never be equalled.

Another serious playwright of the era was Elmer Rice, whose experimental *The Adding Machine* represented a powerful indictment of anti-individualist society. He also wrote on *Trial!; We, the People; The Left Bank, Judgment Day, Cue for Passion!, Counselor-at-Law, The Grand Tour, Flight to the West, The Winner, For the Defense, American Landscape,* his most famous play, *Street Scene* (subsequently a musical with a score by Kurt Weill), and *Dream Girl* in which his wife, Betty Field, starred (later, the musical *Skyscraper*).

Sidney Howard wrote a number of significant, truly American dramas. His *They Knew What They Wanted* (later the musical, *The Most Happy Fella*) won him a Pulitzer Prize in 1925. He also wrote *The Silver Cord; The Bewitched; Casanova; The Ghost of Yankee Doodle; Dodsworth; Yellow Jack; Alien Corn; Lucky Sam McCarver; Madam, Will You Walk; Ned McCobb's Daughter,* and others.

An important dramatist of the twenties and thirties and afterward was Maxwell Anderson, who wrote: *What Price Glory, Elizabeth the Queen, Mary of Scotland, Valley Forge, Winterset, High Tor, Night over Taos, Truckline Cafe, Knickerbocker Holiday, Saturday's Children, Gypsy, Both Your Houses, First Flight, The Masque of Kings, Gods of the Lightning; Cry, the Beloved Country; Joan of Lorraine, Barefoot in Athens, The Bad Seed, Candle in the Wind, The Star-Wagon, The Eve of St. Mark, Ann of the Thousand Days,* and other plays.

Robert Sherwood was a distinguished figure in American drama from the 1930s until the 1950s. He won the Pulitzer Prize no less than four times and authored such memorable works as *The Petrified Forest, Reunion in Vienna, The Queen's Husband, The Road to Rome, There Shall Be No Night, Idiot's Delight, Abe Lincoln in Illinois,* and *Small War on Murray Hill.*

Sidney Kingsley contributed a searing social awareness in his earthy, powerful dramas *Men in White, The Patriots, Dead End, Darkness at Noon, Detective Story. Lunatics and Lovers* and *Night Life,* written somewhat later, reversed his early pattern.

Lillian Hellman commenced her career during the Great Depression. Out of this traumatic period she fashioned a talent that has produced such meaningful works as: *The Children's Hour, Days to Come, The Little Foxes,* and *Another Part of the Forest* (the two plays deal with the rapacious Hubbard family), *Watch on the Rhine,*

Toys in the Attic, The Searching Wind, Montserrat, The Lark; My Mother, My Father, and Me, and *Candide.*

Another important playwright of the Depression was Irwin Shaw, who expressed his sense of outrage at society's inequities in such works as *Bury the Dead, The Gentle People, The Assassin, Patate,* and *Children from Their Games.*

A playwright who verbalized the social unrest and the economic uncertainty of the thirties was Clifford Odets, who contributed such passionate theatrical works as: *Waiting for Lefty, Awake and Sing!, Rocket to the Moon, Night Music, Paradise Lost, Golden Boy, The Country Girl, Clash by Night, The Big Knife,* and *The Flowering Peach* (which later became the musical *Two by Two* starring Danny Kaye).

A few years earlier, George Kelly wrote two memorable satires of middle-class America—*The Show-off* and *Craig's Wife.* His other plays lacked the bite of those enormous successes.

Paul Green wrote several moody, realistic dramas that made a strong theatrical impact on serious playgoers. These include: *In Abraham's Bosom, The House of Connelly,* and *Hymn to the Rising Sun.* His later works, extolling the Old South, stand in complete contrast to his earlier efforts.

John Steinbeck is best known for his prodigious contribution to American literature with such novels as *The Grapes of Wrath* and *The Red Pony.* He did, however, write a magnificent drama, *Of Mice and Men,* which won the 1938 New York Drama Critics Award.

Thornton Wilder wrote three important full-length plays, *Our Town, The Skin of Our Teeth,* and the comedy *The Matchmaker* (originally *The Merchant of Yonkers*), from which the musical *Hello, Dolly!* was fashioned.

William Saroyan deviated between drama and comedy in his efforts for the stage. He wrote such memorable theatre pieces as: *My Heart's in the Highlands; The Time of Your Life; The Cave Dwellers; Get Away Old Man; Hello, Out There; Lily Dafon;* and the aforementioned *Sam, The Highest Jumper of Them All.*

Moving into the 1940s, we encounter two of the most significant dramatists in the history of American theatre, Tennessee Williams and Arthur Miller. Their collective output represents the most impressive array of American drama, second only to the enormous output of Mr. O'Neill.

Williams's works include: *The Glass Menagerie, A Streetcar Named Desire, Cat on a Hot Tin Roof, Summer and Smoke, The Rose Tattoo, Camino Real, Sweet Bird of Youth, Period of Adjustment, Night of the Iguana, The Milk Train Doesn't Stop Here Anymore, Orpheus Descending, The Seven Descents of Myrtle, Slapstick Tragedy,* and, his most recent, *Small Craft Warnings.*

Miller distinguished himself with such memorable theatre pieces as *All My Sons, Death of a Salesman, The Crucible, After the Fall, Incident at Vichy, The Price, A View from the Bridge, A Memory of Two Mondays.* His most recent play is *The Creation of the World and Other Business.*

William Inge, a dramatist in the tradition of Williams, wrote several successful plays in the fifties and sixties, including *Come Back, Little Sheba; Picnic, Bus Stop, The Dark at the Top of the Stairs.* Three other plays, *A Loss of Roses, Natural Affections,* and *Where's Daddy?,* didn't fare as well.

Carson McCullers's tender, poetic *The Member of the Wedding* won the New York Drama Critics Circle Award and introduced a fresh new talent to the American public, the enchanting Julie Harris. Mrs. McCullers's *The Square Root of Wonderful* did not do well at all.

William Gibson contributed *Two for the Seesaw, The Miracle Worker,* and *A Cry of Players.* Robert Anderson wrote *Tea and Sympathy, All Summer Long, I Never Sang for My Father; Silent Night, Holy Night; Dinny and the Witches,* and *I Can't Hear You When the Water's Running.*

Paddy Chayefsky wrote several successful Broadway dramas—*Middle of the Night, The Tenth Man, Gideon,* and two that didn't fare as well, *The Passion of Josef D.* and *The Latent Heterosexual.*

Edward Albee's plays include *Zoo Story, The American Dream, The Death of Bessie Smith, Who's Afraid of Virginia Woolf?, Ballad of the Sad Café, A Delicate Balance, Tiny Alice, Malcolm, The Sand Box, Quotations from Chairman Mao Tse-tung, Everything in the Garden,* and *All Over.*

The poet Archibald MacLeish contributed the religious drama *J.B.* to the American stage. It won the Pulitzer Prize.

Arthur Laurents, now better known for his enormously effective librettos for musical plays, wrote such searing dramas as *The Home of the Brave,* the expressionist *A Clearing in the Woods, The Bird Cage, The Time of the Cuckoo* (later, the musical *Do I Hear a Waltz?*), and *Invitation to a March.*

Dore Schary contributed *Sunrise at Campobello, The Devil's Advocate, The Highest Tree,* and *One by One.*

Robert Ardrey gave us *Thunder Rock, Sing Me No Lullaby,* and *The Shadow of Heroes.*

Jerome Lawrence and Robert E. Lee wrote *Inherit the Wind, The Gang's All Here, Only in America, A Call on Kuprin,* and *The Night Thoreau Spent in Jail.*

Other occasional American dramatists have been: Joseph Hayes, Tad Mosel, James Costigan, Dale Wasserman, Jack Richardson, Jack Gelber, William Hanley, Lewis John Carlino, Arnold Weinstein, Kenneth Brown, Michael Gazzo, James Baldwin, LeRoi Jones, Lorraine Hansberry, John Patrick, Millard Lampell, Sidney Michaels, Ed Bullins, Howard Lackler, Paul Zindel, Charles Gordone, Saul Bellow, David Rayfiel, Frank Gilroy, William Alfred, Ronald Ribman, Megan Terry, Jean-Claude van Itallie, Terrence McNally, Tom Eyen, Rochelle Owens, Kenneth Koch and Israel Horovitz, Leonard Melfi, Sam Shepard, Frederic Knott, David Rabe, Jason Miller, Lucille Fletcher.

Which of these can or will become the Miller, Williams, or Inge of the 1970s and 1980s remains to be seen.

THE BRITISH ARE COMING!

British dramatists who have made an impact on American theatre include: Noel Coward, Terence Rattigan, Graham Greene, Brendan Behan (God forgive me for calling him British), John Osborne (one of the Angry Young Men of the 1950s), Robert Bolt, Arnold Wesker, Shelagh Delaney, Charles Dyer, Tom Stoppard, Joe Orton, Peter Shaffer, Anthony Shaffer (twins), John Whiting, and the latest darling of the theatre aficionados, Harold Pinter, whose menacing, incomprehensible (to many) theatrical excursions have captured the imagination of the "serious" theatregoers. His better-known plays are *The Homecoming, The Birthday Party, The Caretaker,* and *Old Times.*

COMEDY TONIGHT

Comedy is as old as theatre itself. It was the staple of the American stage as early as 1796 when Joe Jefferson I cavorted in the farce *A Budget of Blunders*. Abe Lincoln was shot while watching Laura Keene's popular comedy *Our American Cousin*.

Humpty Dumpty was another early comedic hit. Edward Harrigan, of the comedy team Harrigan and Hart, was a prolific comedy writer.

James M. Barrie wrote some delightful comedies besides his immortal *Peter Pan. What Every Woman Knows* was an immensely popular success. Clyde Fitch wrote a few comedies, although he was best known for his turgid dramas.

Avery Hopwood was a succesful author of farces, the most famous of which was *Getting Gertie's Garter*.

Marc Connelly can be designated a writer of comedies although his most important play was *The Green Pastures*—a kind of fable and not exactly a comedic excursion. His other works, written alone or in collaboration, include: *Dulcy, To The Ladies, Merton of the Movies, Beggar on Horseback, The Farmer Takes a Wife, The Wisdom Tooth, The Wild Man of Borneo, Everywhere I Roam,* and *A Story for Strangers.*

George S. Kaufman is a legend on Broadway. He was, at times, a writer, critic, actor, and director of straight and musical plays. His plays, written alone or with others, include: *I'd Rather Be Right, Of Thee I Sing, Beggar on Horseback, The Royal Family, Dulcy, The Butter and Egg Man, To the Ladies, Merton of the Movies, Once in a Lifetime, You Can't Take It with You, The Man Who Came to Dinner, George Washington Slept Here, The Fabulous Invalid, The American Way; Merrily, We Roll Along; The Solid Gold Cadillac, First Lady, Let 'Em Eat Cake, The Cocoanuts, Strike Up the Band,* and many others.

Moss Hart wrote a number of spectacularly successful comedies and musical comedy books, alone or in collaboration. His plays include: *Once in a Lifetime, You Can't Take It with You, The Man Who Came to Dinner, The Fabulous Invalid, The American Way, Merrily We Roll Along, Face the Music, As Thousands Cheer, Jubi-*

lee, *Lady in the Dark, Winged Victory, Light up the Sky, I'd Rather Be Right, Miss Liberty,* and *The Climate of Eden.*

S. N. Behrman is the master of the sophisticated comedy. His efforts include: *The Second Man, Meteor, Biography, End of Summer, Wine of Choice, Rain from Heaven, Brief Moment, No Time for Comedy, The Talley Method, Amphitryon 38, Jacobowsky and the Colonel, Serena Blandish, I Know My Love, The Cold Wind and the Warm, But For Whom Charlie, Dunnigan's Daughter, Lord Pengo,* and *Fanny.*

Philip Barry wrote comedies and dramas. Some of his better-known plays are: *The Philadelphia Story, In a Garden, Paris Bound, White Wings, Hotel Universe, You and I, The Youngest, Tomorrow and Tomorrow, The Animal Kingdom, Here Come the Clowns, Liberty Jones, The Joyous Season,* and *Second Threshold.*

Sam and Bella Spewack were a successful husband and wife comedy writing team. Some of their plays were: *Boy Meets Girl, Leave It to Me, Kiss Me Kate, My 3 Angels, Clear All Wires, Two Blind Mice, Under the Sycamore Tree, Woman Bites Dog,* and *Miss Swan Expects.*

Howard Lindsay and Russel Crouse wrote such memorable hits as *Life With Father, State of the Union, Life with Mother, The Great Sebastians, Anything Goes; Red, Hot and Blue; Hooray for What!, Call Me Madam, The Sound of Music, Mr. President,* and *Tall Story.*

Samuel Taylor has contributed *Sabrina Fair, The Happy Time, The Pleasure of His Company, Beekman Place, First Love,* and *Avanti!*

Ronald Alexander wrote *The Grand Prize, Holiday for Lovers, Nobody Loves an Albatross.*

John Van Druten wrote *I Remember Mama, I Am a Camera, The Damask Cheek, The Voice of the Turtle; Bell, Book and Candle; Young Woodley* and other brilliant comedies.

George Axelrod made his mark with *Seven Year Itch, Will Success Spoil Rock Hunter?,* and *Goodbye, Charlie.*

Murray Schisgal made a small sensation with his modern comedy, *Luv.* His other efforts include *Jimmy Shine, The Typists, The Tiger, Ducks and Lovers, Knit One, Purl One,* and *Windows.*

Bruce Jay Friedman has written *Scuba-Duba* and *A Mother's Kisses.*

Neil Simon is probably the most successful comedy playwright of all time. His brilliant record includes: *Come Blow Your Horn, Barefoot in the Park, The Odd Couple, Plaza Suite, Sweet Charity, Little Me; Promises, Promises; Star Spangled Girl, The Gingerbread Lady, The Prisoner of Second Avenue, The Last of the Red Hot Lovers,* and his most recent, *The Sunshine Boys.*

Other comedy writers on and off Broadway have been: F. Hugh Herbert, Norman Krasna, Harry Kurnitz, Garson Kanin, Gore Vidal, Joseph Fields and Jerome Chodorov, John Cecil Holm, Ruth Gordon, Ben Hecht and Charles MacArthur, Frederick Lonsdale, Leonard Spigelgass, Jean Kerr, Clare Booth, Muriel Resnik, Howard Teichmann, Norman Barasch and Carroll Moore, Herb Gardner, Arnold Schulman, Carl Reiner, Henry Denker, Peter Ustinov, Ira Levin, Mary Chase, Woody Allen, and Elaine May.

DIRECTORS

Directors of straight plays on and off Broadway are and have been:

Alan Schneider
Ulu Grosbard
Jack Garfein
Mike Nichols
Elia Kazan (to be really *in*, call him Gadge)
Arthur Penn
Lloyd Richards
William Ball
Harold Clurman
Lee Strasberg
George S. Kaufman
Jed Harris
Orson Welles
Cheryl Crawford
Philip Moeller
John Houseman
Guthrie McClintic

John Gielgud
Joshua Logan
Gene Saks
Arthur Storch
Robert Lewis
Gerald Freedman
André Gregory
José Quintero
Joseph Anthony
Peter Koss
Fred Coe
Michael Bennett
Tyrone Guthrie
Howard da Silva
Peter Hall
Peter Brook
Michael Langham
Robert Moore

José Ferrer
John Hancock
Michael Kahn

Stuart Vaughan, and many, many others.

The really *big* names in theatre direction are Stanislavski, Max Reinhardt, Erwin Piscator, Margaret Webster, Vsevolod Meyerhold, Louis Jouvet, Jean-Louis Barrault, Joan Littlewood, and Jerzy Grotowski.

SCENIC DESIGNERS

Some of the good ones are or have been:

Jo Mielziner
Boris Aronson
Robert Edmond Jones
Oliver Smith
Lee Simonson
Norman Bel Geddes
Donald Oenslager
Gordon Craig
Woodman Thompson
Aline Bernstein
Rollo Peters
Lemuel Ayres

Howard Bay
Ming Che Lee
Robert Randolph
William and Jean Eckart
Tony Walton
Raoul Pène du Bois
Rouben Ter-Arutunian
Lloyd Burlingame
Sam Love
Ralph Alswang
William Ritman

LIGHTING DESIGNERS

Many of the abovementioned scenic designers also double as lighting directors. A few others are or were: Jules Fisher, Abe Feder, Jean Rosenthal, Tharon Musser, Martin Aronstein, Peggy Clark, and Will Steven Armstrong.

COSTUME DESIGNERS

A few of the good ones are or were:

Irene Sharoff
Freddy Wittop

Motley
Alvin Colt

Noel Taylor   Lucinda Ballard
Theoni V. Aldredge   Patton Campbell
Winn Morton   Miles White
Jane Greenwood   David Ffolkes
Patricia Zipprodt   Adrian
Raoul Pène du Bois   Donald Brooks
Cecil Beaton

PRODUCERS

Following the Frohmans, Ziegfeld, and Belasco, the most famous
producers since the beginning of the century have been: The Shu-
berts, Gilbert Miller, Arthur Hopkins, Sam Harris, Winthrop Ames,
Charles Dillingham, Al Woods, Brock Pemberton, Max Gordon,
Morris Gest, John Golden, and several group efforts—namely The
Theater Guild, Actors Studio, The Playwrights Company, and the
celebrated Group Theater, an offshoot of the Theater Guild, which
gave rise to such stellar talents as Elia (Gadge) Kazan, John Garfield,
Luther Adler, Clifford Odets, Frances Farmer, Cheryl Crawford,
Franchot Tone, Morris Carnovsky, Stella Adler, Lee J. Cobb, San-
ford Meisner, Boris Aronson, and others.

Other producers have included:

Billy Rose   Fred Coe
Mike Todd   Frederick Brisson
Herman Shumlin   Robert Whitehead
Kermit Bloomgarden   Alexander Cohen
Joseph Hyman   Harold Prince
Leland Hayward   Saint Subber
Feuer and Martin   Herman Levin
Fryer and Carr   David Merrick
Joseph Kipness   Dwight Deere Wiman
Vinton Freedley   Alfred de Liagre, Jr.
Herman Shumlin

MORE STARS

Names that have glittered in comedy and drama on Broadway
include:

Charles Coburn
Dudley Digges
Katharine Cornell
George Arliss
Edward Arnold
Tallulah Bankhead
Gertrude Berg
Charles Bickford
Sidney Blackmer
Mary Boland
Shirley Booth
Claude Rains
Cornelia Otis Skinner
Helen Hayes
Judith Anderson
Lionel Atwill
Paul Muni
James Barton
Cedric Hardwicke
Fredric March
Jane Cowl
Spencer Tracy
Louis Calhern
Basil Rathbone
Charles Boyer
Barry Nelson
Raymond Massey
Marlon Brando
Edward J. Bromberg
Yul Brynner
Howard da Silva
Walter Hampden
Leora Dana
Noel Coward
Charles Laughton
Lillian and Dorothy Gish
Grace George
Julie Haydon
Leo Genn

Dennis King
Billie Burke
Florence Eldridge
Ralph Meeker
Joseph Schildkraut
Edith Evans
George C. Scott
Maurice Evans
Kim Hunter
Arthur Kennedy
Alice Brody
Elaine Strich
Margaret Sullavan
Deborah Kerr
Ina Claire
Ruth Chatterton
Colleen Dewhurst
Henry Fonda
Alexander Knox
George Coulouris
Jeanne Eagels
Eleanora Duse
Alfred Lunt and
    Lynn Fontanne
Frank Craven
Tyrone Power
Eva Le Gallienne
Josephine Hull
Rip Torn
Margaret Leighton
Walter Huston
Eli Wallach
Viveca Lindfors
Sylvia Sidney
Tom Ewell
Kim Stanley
Frank Fay
Gene Lockhart
Uta Hagen

Aline MacMahon	Pauline Lord
Julie Harris	Geraldine Page
Paul Lukas	Ruth Gordon
Hume Cronyn	James Stewart
Burgess Meredith	Jessica Tandy
Eileen Heckart	Edward G. Robinson
Jack Albertson	Nazimova
Art Carney	Lenore Ulric
David Warfield	Barbara Harris
Sam Levene	Christopher Plummer
Maureen Stapleton	Paul Newman
Michael O'Sullivan	Laurence Olivier
Barbara Loden	Mitchell Ryan
Ben Gazzara	Rosemary Harris
Menasha Skulnik	Jason Robards, Jr.
Blanche Yurka	Walter Mathau
May Robson	Martha Scott
Charles Winninger	Lucile Watson
Salome Jens	Roland Young
Pat Hingle	Louis Wolheim
Katharine Hepburn	Barbara Bel Geddes
Paul Ford	

Irene Worth, and dozens and dozens of other talented people.

CRITICS

Important critics in the theatre have been: George Jean Nathan, Alexander Woollcott, Percy Hammond, Burns Mantle, Brooks Atkinson, John Anderson, John Mason Brown, Elliot Norton, Walter Kerr, Robert Garland, Robert Coleman, Ward Morehouse, Richard Watts, Howard Barnes, Robert Benchley, John Chapman, and Clive Barnes.

OFF-BROADWAY AND OFF-OFF-BROADWAY

The powerful Off-Broadway movement peaked in the 1960s. Today, things are as rough Off Broadway as they are on.

A few better known Off- and Off-Off-Broadway enterprises are, or have been:

The Lincoln Center Repertory Theater directed by Jules Irving, which occasionally fizzles to life, then quietly goes back to sleep again.

The Phoenix Theatre which for a time combined with the Association of Producing Artists, or APA. Ellis Rabb directed the APA and Edward Hambleton ran the Phoenix. The current status of both groups can, at the moment, be best described as fluid.

The American Place Theater under the direction of Wynn Handman seems to be going strong in its new home on West 46th Street in New York City.

The New York Shakespeare Festival Public Theater under the dynamic Joe Papp is flourishing, both in its home base, on Broadway, and in Central Park.

The Negro Ensemble Company is going on.

The Roundabout Theater is bravely keeping its head above water.

The LaMaMa Experimental Theatre Club under Ellen Stewart is hanging in there.

The Living Theater run by Julian Beck and Judith Malina is dead.

The Open Theater run by Joseph Chaikin is closed.

The American Shakespeare Festival at Stratford, Connecticut, is moving right along.

The Arena Stage in Washington, D.C., is still alive.

There is some action at the Mercer-Hansberry Theatre.

The McCarter Theatre of Princeton University is keeping on.

There is a New Jersey Shakespeare Festival in New Jersey.

The straw-hat circuit is alive and flourishing with theatres cropping up like mushrooms all over Long Island, New Jersey, Pennsylvania, Connecticut, Massachusetts, Maine, Vermont, New Hampshire, and everywhere.

Yale University Repertory Theater is thriving under Robert Brustein's care.

Circle-in-the-Square under Theodore Mann and Paul Libin is moving uptown.

There are festivals all over the map—the Lenox Arts Festival, The Shaw Festival, the Festival of American Theatre, and what not.

Regional theatre is strongly entrenched, with permanent companies in most major cities in the country.

Even the Yiddish theatre, which has been "dying" for forty years, manages to mount productions here and there.

In the meantime, the various churches, garages, supermarkets, and lofts that have been converted into acting companies—most bearing pretentious names—are still proliferating in and around New York City. American theatre lives!

ADDENDA

The more things change the more they stay the same. Sardi's is still the prime hangout for theatre buffs and professionals. Other *in* spots in New York where you might encounter theatre folk are: The Gaiety Delicatessen, Joe Allen's, Frankie and Johnnie, Delsomma, Broadway Joe's Steak House, Clarke's Bar, and Downey's Steak House.

Happy bluffing.